A Purple Heart Bride

Published by

Angel Publications

Trade Paperback

This novel is historical fiction

Published December 2015

Copyright 2015 Daniel W. Stuart

Cover art Copyright 2015 Daniel W. Stuart

ISBN 978-09881628-4-6

This book is dedicated to the peace keepers; meaning all those who protect freedom and fight against oppression and corruption. Special thanks to our military and police forces without whom we would live in anarchy. To those who would try to oppress corrupt or enslave,,, may the Lord God deal with you most swiftly.

A Purple Heart Bride

Preface

Several years ago while visiting my brother in Saskatchewan, he toured me around the Weyburne airport and what during world war two was the alternate airfield in Albright.. It was interesting because I was told that not only did my dad work as a plumber installing the plumbing there, but he worked for my uncle, who was the contractor for many aerodromes, as the airports were called at the time. My imagination was suddenly alive with pictures of military airmen crisscrossing between the giant hangers. Weyburne and many other like aerodromes were the training grounds for Allied Air-Forces. As I toured the buildings trying to figure out what each one had been used for, my resolve to write this novel grew.

One thing I would like to point out is that this is meant to be a historical fiction, due to the fact the places were in real and some of the people were real. I like to quote a famous author who said in books the only difference between non-fiction and fiction is that the fiction novel has to be more believable. I hope you enjoy this novel as much as I had researching and writing it.

Shalom!

The Purple Heart Bride
Chapter 1

Charles Lysik and his wife, Veronica acquired land through the Dominion land grant in 1920 for the ten dollars administration fee and moved to the wilderness of central Saskatchewan to start a new home. Charles and Veronica worked long days to clear 50 acres of the quarter section, build a log shack and planted a garden the first summer. The following year, Charles applied for and got another three quarters of land adjacent to their property. The Lysik farm now consisted of one section of land. Of the 640 acres, 400 was woodlot. There was even a small lake bordering the farm.

David was the first son to be born a year after they arrived and thus the family started to grow. During the following six years, Charles and his wife were blessed with three more boys: John, George and Ezekiel. Many years of hard work followed, during which the couple often contemplated leaving the farm and moving to a more sedentary life, but there was always that something - neither of them could properly describe it - that urged them to stay and face the next year.

As the years went by and the boys began to reach an age where they could help with the farm work, the load on the two began to lighten, and life became a little more pleasurable.

By the time David reached 12, he was doing the work of a grown man and John, although a year younger, was doing nearly the same amount. Generally, as George and Ezekiel played or helped Veronica with some of the house chores, Charles, David and John took care of all the outdoor farm chores.

David, when he had some free time, enjoyed hiking to the woodlot on the far side of the farm where he had found a special place in a stand of large spruce trees. It was a nice spot where the floor of the forest was clear of shrubs due to the lack of sunlight and the abundance of spruce needles. He would go there and feel quiet and close to nature. He had given his heart to the Lord and became a Christian there. He had also found that this spot was the perfect place to have heart-to-heart talks with his Lord.

One hot July day as he sat there on a log, a squirrel began chattering loudly. Dave tried to put the noise out of his mind, thinking that the little creature was taking offense to his proximity.

"You just go mind your own business," Dave said with a chuckle. It was then he heard the low guttural growl of another beast. He slowly turned toward the sound and saw a cougar sprawled on a lower branch of a large spruce tree just a short distance away. The big cat was slowly beginning to position himself into a stance that would allow him to catapult the short distance to Dave. Dave slowly moved his hand down to his Bowie knife that he carried in a sheath attached to his belt and undid the leather strap that held the knife in. At the same time, with his other hand, he reached for his Winchester 30-30, not making any sudden moves. Moments went by as the two sat facing each other. They were eye-to-eye tense moments. Dave, with steady deliberation, brought the rifle to the ready as the big cat reached a position from which he could spring.

"Lord, if I ever needed you, this is the time. Help me Lord," he prayed in a whisper." Dave was just ready to squeeze off a shot when the cat suddenly lurched the other way and literally ran down the tree and away. It was then that Dave heard some twigs break somewhere behind him and turned quickly to see what could possibly have scared the cougar away. He was surprised to catch a glimpse of his father walking up the path.

"Hey dad, did you see that cougar?" Dave shouted.

"No. Where was he?"

"Up on that branch over there." Dave pointed to the tree. "The squirrel was the one that tried to alert me first and then I heard the cougar's growl. I'm pretty sure he was ready to spring and then he just whipped around and took off," Dave said excitedly.

"We'll have to watch out for him - maybe keep Bessie and the other animals in the barn for a while." Charles said. Dave gave his father an inquisitive look.

"What are you doing out here anyway, Dad?"

"You think you're the only one that knows about this spot? I've spent time here nearly every Sunday before we got the church built over at Christopher Lake. It was the one place I could come to be truly alone with the Lord, but now I guess I'll have to share it." He grinned with a look of total pride at his boy.

"You'd better un-cock that rifle and do up your sheath. Wouldn't want any accidents happening," Charles chuckled.

XXXXXXXXXXXXXXXXXXXXXXXXXXXXXXXXXXXXXXXXXXXXXXX

The Dirty Thirties moved into the center of the decade and the North American "Bread Bowl" became more and more the "Dust Bowl". Many farmers to the south had to give up their land and try to compete in more urban areas, while others moved from town to town by jumping freight trains. There was little work, of course and it wasn't uncommon for a man to do any type of arduous chores just for a meal. Many of the farms further north had it somewhat easier, but it was a time of disparity for all. At the same time, there began to be rumblings of a more sinister type in Europe. An Austrian-born German corporal from World War 1 was stirring up discontent about the Jews and other ethnic groups, using it to cement his rise to power in Germany. This news from

Europe troubled Charles and Veronica, due to the fact that they were Jewish by birth and, although they had converted to Christianity, they nonetheless considered themselves Jewish.

They followed the news of Europe and especially that of Germany and Hitler. They also listened for anything that a little-known member of British parliament and Lord of the Admiralty - Winston Churchill - had to say. He was the one who had advocated stopping Adolf Hitler before he had done too much damage. As they sat in the living room listening to the American program, The Jack Benny Show, via CBC radio on Sept 10, 1939, Canada's own Prime Minister, McKenzie King broke in with a special announcement. Canada was following Britain's lead and declaring war with Nazi Germany.

Although the Lysik family was not happy about war and all the awful things attributed to it, they were happy that their country was going to fight this maniac of evil who had already caused so much destruction and heartache. Dave had already decided on his course of action. He would join the RAF and become a fighter pilot.

Charles was successful at dissuading Dave for a very long time, but he could only postpone the inevitable and Dave decided that he must sign up. Victoria became very emotional about the plan.

"But Mom, I have to. I know I will be a great pilot and I know I will love flying!" Dave said in

9

earnest.

"I didn't raise you to see you shot down and killed in Europe," she cried. "Why can't we just live our lives that your father and I have worked so hard for?"

"Because if we don't stop this - this Hitler thug, no one will have the life they have worked for." David was more direct than he had ever been with his mother before, but without belligerence. Charles put his arm around his wife and tried to console her.

"The boy is 18 and he needs to do this, Vicky. Let him go." She leaned into her husband's chest as tears flowed down her cheeks. She gave in, feeling that she was outnumbered.

So it was that in November of 1939, Dave drove the family's "38" Ford truck to Prince Albert and enlisted.

xxxxxxxxxxxxxxxxxxxxxxxxxxxxxxxxxxxxxxxxxx

It was December and the Saskatchewan winter was in full swing when Dave got his orders to report to Prince Albert for medicals and indoctrination. Shortly afterwards, he was sent to the Elementary Flying School at the Prince Albert Airport, for introduction of flight training. It was there that he saw a friend from Christopher Lake in the mess hall.

"George Waters, you son-of-a-gun. What the heck are you doing here?"

George swung around, knowing Dave by his voice. "Hey, Dave, I wondered if you'd show up.

I'm gonna try and get into fighter planes."

"That's great," Dave said. "I am too." At that moment, the buzzer went off and it was their cue to head for classes.

"Hey, I'll catch you later, George. I'm in class down the hall in room 15."

"Yeah, I'm doing maintenance in the hanger. Maybe we can get together later," George replied, as he hurried off in the opposite direction of Dave.

They did meet each other a lot over the following months, but soon their fifty hours of flight time was completed, and George and Dave were boarding a train headed south for Weyburn, Saskatchewan.

As the train jostled from side to side in a rhythmic motion, Dave's mind strayed to the day he had enlisted and recalled one of the first questions the recruiting officer had asked.

"Why do you want to join the RCAF?" a lieutenant with meticulously pressed uniform asked.

"When I was 10, my dad bought me a ticket at the fair and I got to ride in a tiger moth" Dave said, without hesitation. "I felt it had to be the next best thing to heaven and ever since then, I've wanted to be a pilot." He became somewhat somber and continued. "Besides, my uncle was in the Great War and he told me about the way things were in the trenches. The rain, mud, rats and terrible conditions almost made going over the top and getting shot a blessing. He told me more troops died from disease than from the Hun's bullets." By the smile that the lieutenant had given him, Dave reasoned that he must have given a good answer and now here he was, about to become a fighter pilot.

Dave's thoughts now turned to some of the other young recruits on the train who, just like he, had recently finished the basic training and the fifty hours flying time in Elementary Flying School. Some had come directly from other facilities, but most of them would be transferred to the Service Flying Training School at Weyburn. He mused about flying the Tiger Moth back at P.A. and now getting into the Harvard AT6, which was one of the normal progressions in training for fighter pilots. A familiar voice from the back of the coach broke Dave's reverie.

"Hey Dave, what's the matter? You afraid this crate is going to crash?" It was George, and the remark caused a few snickers.

"No," Dave replied. "Not as long as we're not in a plane and you're not flying it." That brought a guffaw from George and a boisterous round of laughter from the others, temporarily silencing the heckler.

Dave noticed that the train was slowing and, due to the fact that they had already made the Regina stop, he figured it must be Weyburn. When the train had lurched several times and then come to a stop, the boys exited and then a burly sergeant ordered them to line up near the tracks. They were almost in position when the sergeant yelled, "A ten hun!" in a voice that several thought could crack cement. Immediately, the young men came to attention with all discussions ceased. It was then that they saw the major.

"At ease men." The noise of even the little town seemed to evaporate. "Good morning, gentlemen. I am Major Arthur Jameson. I am responsible for your training here for the next sixteen weeks. Eighteen of you have been evaluated as potential fighter pilots and thus will be trained on the North American Harvard. Some of the rest will begin training on twin engines, like the Avro Anson over there." He pointed up the hill, indicating the airport. We welcome you and hope you learn well. I will leave you in the capable hands of the sergeant here to get you to the airport and then we will get to the business at hand. He motioned for the sergeant to take over.

The sergeant stepped up and said, with the same booming voice as before, "Alright, in single file. We will now give the fine people of Weyburn a show as we march to our barracks. You will follow me in proper order and in step." The men did their very best to proudly march in unison, and they couldn't help noticing the locals watching.

Once they were at the airport and inside the third of several gigantic hangers, Major Jameson directed the men's attention to a twin-engine aircraft in the far corner.

"We call them Faithful Annies because they always seem to get their crew back home, but make no mistake, you are the ones who will either get them back or crash. The Avro has also been dubbed the flying greenhouse due to the fact that their fuselage is largely constructed of plywood and the cockpit has the large Plexiglas windscreens." He stopped for a second. "Forty-five of you will learn to pilot the Annies and as I said before, eighteen will pilot the Harvard AT-6. The remainder will train as crew members, practising communications, navigation and weapons." The major could see some consternation and some wide grins. "When you have completed your training here, and if you pass, which most of you will, you will either be transferred to other training facilities or sent off to England. Are there any questions?"

The officer gazed around at a group of bright young kids who, at the end of the time he had just described, could be flying over the English Channel in Spitfires, Hurricanes, Lancasters or a dozen other types of war planes, taking the fight to the Germans.

"To the north and south of us," he continued, "are two other hangers just like this one. Fighter groups, that is the AT-6's will be in hanger number two, with schoolroom training upstairs; twin engine will be here in number three. In one will be a classroom for Navigation and

Communication Training. The mess hall and barracks are directly west of us and the dance hall is in Weyburn down near the Souris River, one and a half miles southwest of the barracks." At that, there was a round of applause, with cat whistles and hooting.

"All right now, settle down. It'll be some time before you get leave, so you'll have to learn to curb your enthusiasm for extracurricular cultural affairs." He raised his eyebrows and grinned as he noticed, by the look on the young recruits' faces, that only half of them caught his meaning, but knew as well that it wouldn't be an enigma for the less-informed group for long. "I will now introduce Captain John Martin. He and his men will be your instructors here. Listen to them and do everything they say- it could mean your very life or that of your fellow airmen. Captain, take over and get these men squared away." Captain Martin, a tall lean man in perfect uniform, quickly turned to his subordinates.

"All right, men, divide these fellows into their groups and get them settled. Have them in their appointed classrooms at fourteen hundred hours for their first briefing." The corporals gave a quick tour of the training base and when they reached the barracks, each man was assigned a cot and footlocker and was told to stow their belongings. As the corporal was about to leave, he swung around at the door.

"It's now 12:30 hours. I will be back at 13:45 to

pick you up for your first session. I suggest you grab a shower, have a snack at the mess hall and be ready when I get here." Everyone snapped to attention in their best military form.

"Yes Sir!" they collectively yelled.

After the corporal left, George shuffled over to Dave.

"So when we get leave are we gonna go find some girls?" George asked.

"I don't know. It won't be for at least a few weeks and even then…" Dave trailed off as he noticed his friend fidgeting. "What about Bonnie? You asked her to wait for you didn't you? And besides, I came here to learn to fly, not learn to date." Dave gave a little chuckle. "You know how I get choked up around girls." George rolled his eyes.

"First of all good buddy, Bonnie was already going steady with that wimp Tim Shier before we left to sign up and second I think you need some real pilot training. A true pilot ought to be able to fly one of these babies with a girl on each knee." Dave chuckled again, but this time at his friend's absurd observation.

"Yeah, well all I can say is don't let the instructors catch you. I think they'd take a dim view of civilians riding in their planes, especially on the pilot's knees." George eyed Dave suspiciously.

"Don't you want to find a girl and go dancing and stuff?"

"Of course, but later on - right now, I just want to learn to be the best damned pilot here."

"Dave, Dave, you've got your priorities all turned around," George said, waving him off. "First you have fun and then if you still have some time, you apply it to flying. Get it?"

"No," Dave said becoming irritated. "I don't get it. I'm going to put my all into my training and if I get through it, then maybe I'll find a girl. Anyway, we had better get ready; that corporal will be here before you know it."

The guys got cleaned up and had a snack by the time the corporal arrived to escort them to their classroom in hanger two. Dave, George and another five with them joined other groups training on the Harvards in the giant building. As soon as all the men had assembled, a sergeant began the first lecture beside one of the planes.

"Boys, this is the Harvard AT6," the instructor said, motioning to the shiny new yellow plane with the Canadian Roundel on it. "Listen to us and do exactly what we tell you because if you make one mistake, you could be dead. There's just no room for guessing. Secondly, these babies cost twenty-seven thousand dollars each. They are the fastest, most powerful trainer of their size in Canada and will do over two hundred miles per hour." At this, the sergeant motioned for the recruits to climb up and see the cockpit. Dave gazed at the controls and his eyes fixed on the speedometer. He smiled as he saw it swept all the way up to 300 miles per hour. He stared at all the other gauges and controls.

How on earth does anyone fly that fast and keep track of all this? he wondered.

When the last man had returned to his seat, the Sergeant continued.

"If you noticed the speedometer, you saw the big 300. You'll probably cruise around 180 and that's going to feel fast, but when and if you slip into a Spitfire, you'll find them twice as powerful and twice as fast as these. The Spitfire can top 350 mph. So learn your lessons well and practice at every opportunity, because when you do start flying the Spitfires or Hurricanes, there'll soon enough be a Messerschmidt on your tail. That's when you'll need all the skill you can bring to bear." He then began going into the more technical specifications of the Harvard.

For the next few weeks, Dave and the others went through all the numbers, tolerances, formations and manoeuvres over and over again. Their instructor showed them every gauge, dial lever and switch in the aircraft to the point that most of the men could recite the lessons word for word. Some of them did, to mock the instructor, but only when they knew they were out of earshot of the officer. Dave even dreamed of the sessions, but in an abstract way.

It was a short three weeks later that Dave was in the pilot's seat of the AT6, doing his first solo flight. He taxied out to runway three six and a green flare was the indicator for take-off. He lined up on the runway. *"I can do this,"* he thought almost out loud. Quickly he glanced through the myriad of gauges and switches to ensure he hadn't missed anything. He hadn't. He pulled the throttle to one quarter and as the engine spooled up he felt the fuselage vibrate. He then pulled it to three quarters as he released the brake. The Harvard quickly picked up speed and inside a few seconds, Dave pulled back on the stick and his wheels left the asphalt. He retracted the landing gear, returned flaps to zero and set the trim while proceeding with a textbook climb.

To Dave, this was a dream come true. He flew the Harvard following the given flight plan, holding altitude and performing the required manoeuvres for his flight. When he had accomplished his orders, he brought the noisy plane around to the final leg and approach. He cut power, lowered flaps and pulled the lever for the landing gear, noticing the tiny green landing gear light come on as he proceeded to land the plane.

Had Dave been a seasoned pilot, he may have realized that the wheels had not locked. He might have then tried to take the aircraft up and shake it a bit, thereby loosening up the latch so that the struts locked or even run through lowering and raising the gear a few times to help it happen. He may have even decided to emergency belly-land the plane on the snow without lowering the gear, but he wasn't seasoned and as far as he knew, everything was running exactly the way it was supposed to.

His instructor watched in horror as the wheels, not perpendicular to the fuselage, touched the asphalt and as the weight of the plane transferred onto them, they collapsed. The nose and propeller skidded along the runway, showering sparks until the plane veered off into the gravel, where a wing gouged into the dirt and the plane cartwheeled, coming to rest upside down - a pile of twisted metal in the infield.

Men appeared from everywhere running toward the crash scene. The emergency services, in a 1937 Ford fire truck and a 1935 white panel van with a giant red cross on the sides, rushed out onto the infield and began trying to extricate the young pilot. After twenty minutes of tearing with a crowbar, bashing with a sledge hammer and even using the fire truck to hook onto a chunk of the plane with a chain and tearing it off, they managed to get to Dave, who by this time was barely alive. His face and flight suit were covered with his own blood and both legs and arms were hanging in macabre angles. The rescue team had to be careful due to the fact that he was hanging in the seat restraint upside down. He never regained consciousness as he was extricated and laid on a gurney. The men quickly slid the stretcher into the ambulance and with sirens blaring and red light flashing, it whisked him away

through town and up the hill to the Weyburn
hospital. No one expected him to live.

The Purple Heart Bride
Chapter 2

Dave was immediately taken to an emergency room on the ground floor where a young nurse named Julia Burrs checked his injuries. As she went through the ABC's, she realized that she was finding far too many. His airway was partially obstructed, his breathing was very shallow and there were so many lacerations that even with the field dressings the airbase medics had applied, he was still losing much too much blood.

"Isn't there any doctor in the hospital? This man needs one right now," she spoke in the direction of the head nurse. The older nurse was getting supplies that they would need.

"Julia, we tried. Doctor Jones is in Regina and Doctor Reynolds is out at the Carter place. I sent the young Davies boy out to get him, so we'll just have to do the best we can till he gets here."

Julia checked Dave's breathing and found that it was getting shallower. This led her to further check for wounds in the thoracic area and sure enough, after removing his shirt, she found a sucking chest wound. Working quickly, she taped a square piece of plastic with a hole in the centre over the wound. Then over that she taped a second square of plastic and sealed it on three sides. She was happy to see that it acted as a one-way valve. When he breathed out, some of the air that had entered the chest cavity between the lung and the outer wall was expelled, but when he breathed in, the plastic sealed the wound. Julia watched the area closely as she cleaned other wounds as best she could. The head nurse was, meanwhile, monitoring his vital signs, which to Julia's joy began to improve slightly.

Doctor Reynolds, arrived about an hour later and began a thorough assessment, but after discovering the severity of his many injuries, came to the opinion that the young man had a slim chance of surviving. After consulting with the head nurse, he made his way over to Julia.

"That valve on the chest wound is the only reason this boy is still alive. You did an excellent job on it. If he responds over the night, we might replace it with a thoracic drain. Do you know how to rig that?" Julia nodded and the doctor continued to scan the young man's wounds.

"Nurse, I'm going to suture these flesh wounds, but not set the fractures right now. If the young man shows any recovery over the next 24 hours, I'll consider performing some surgery when he gains enough strength. The best we can do for him right now is to administer morphine and try to make him comfortable."

The nurses were to check his condition every 15 minutes through the long night, but Julia took a special interest in him and hardly left his room. By morning, the other hospital staff began to suspect that there was more to her vigilance than just nurses' duties and they became concerned about the effect it would have on her when the young pilot didn't make it.

Julia's check of the young man was careful and thorough. She started with the head laceration. She followed it across the side of his head, making sure that none of the stitches were being pulled. Next, she checked the chest wound to ensure that the lung was draining properly and the air and blood were properly exhausting. She finished her examination, ensuring that the broken arms and legs were in a safe position. The first day, she was in the young pilot's room most of the day and though, by the end of her shift, she thought she was seeing an improvement, the head nurse disagreed with her.

The second day, she was certain that he was getting better and when his respiration and blood pressure began to somewhat stabilize, she happily wrote the improvements of his vital signs into his chart. Julia finished her shift and felt as light as a feather as she finally left the hospital. It was a feeling that she had helped to heal the young man in some way, but somehow it seemed more than that.

By the third day, Dave had started to improve so much that Doctor Reynolds decided to begin operating on the fractures. He would set, pin, wire and splint them, as well as correct the many other injuries. The operating room and the young pilot were prepped and the surgery began. Doctor

Reynolds had not specialize in surgery, so he assisted a specialist brought in from Regina. They spent the next seven hours bent over the young flyer, with Julia and other nurses helping. They set and pinned the right shoulder, wired the boy's jaw in three places and then worked down to the chest and closed off the thoracic injury. Next, they began work on the neck of the femur which was dislocated; they placed it back in its socket and then set and splinted both lower legs that were broken in several places. Finally, they operated on his right arm which had been fractured in three different bones - the radius, ulna and the upper arm. They completed the surgery and took one last observation.

The physicians were exhausted by the time they finished. They almost stumbled out of the operating room with their surgical aprons covered with the young man's blood. Doctor Reynolds smiled as they washed up.

"Nurse Burrs," he nodded toward the recovery room. "That boy owes you his life. I intend to write a letter of commendation for you." Julia felt somewhat embarrassed as she felt her face flush red, but didn't say anything. "He's a strong young man, but I don't hold much hope that he'll be able to walk again," Reynolds added. Julia felt her heart stop.

"Of course he will walk again," she thought. Julia stayed in the recovery area watching her patient. More than an hour later, Dave temporarily regained consciousness. The first thing he saw when he opened his eyes was the young nurse.

"A I in heaben?" he said in a morphine-induced slur. He stared at her, trying to focus. "I tink I gonna like it here. I comfortable and I got anels taking care a me."

Julia smiled at him as her face went red again.

"Well don't get too comfortable fly boy, because this isn't heaven and I'm no angel." She snickered at the thought. "This is a hospital and we're going to get you well and back in the air." At that moment, their eyes locked and even in his semi-conscious state, those inner bells, whistles and sirens went off full blast. Julia felt it too, but broke the trance.

"Okay, you get some rest and I'll check in on you in a little while." Dave tried to gaze at her as long as he could, but his eyelids grew heavy and finally closed. He drifted into an unconscious state, dreaming of a beautiful angel and heaven for another eighteen hours.

When he awoke and opened his eyes, he gazed around the room and finally managed to focus on the angel. The room was different, but she was still here. Julia had actually gone home and returned for her next normal shift.

"I was beginning to think that you were just a dream and I wouldn't see you anymore." He said although the words were still slurred due to the wired up jawbone and the morphine. Julia smiled and tucked the bed sheet under his mattress.

"Are you still under the influence of the medication or are you always this aggressive?"

"It must be the morphine because I'm usually real shy around beautiful women."

"You think I'm beautiful huh?" Julia asked with a snicker.

"Honestly, when I woke up before, I thought you were an angel and I was in heaven and I wasn't at all unhappy about it. It's kind of a kick in the teeth that it wasn't heaven, but here you are, still here in real life." Julia straightened up a nightstand across the room and fidgeted with anything she could find, trying to act as though she didn't hear what the patient was saying.

She couldn't quite figure out why she felt that she had to take good care of this guy - she just knew she had to. She, in fact took such good care of him, that she managed a reprimand from the head matron for not keeping up with some of her other routine duties.

Dave's condition responded accordingly and in three weeks he was out of bed with crutches moving around the hospital. The ever-present Julia was always by his side to help steady and encourage him during his exercise. Day by day, a deep love for each other began to blossom, which was also a further elixir for Dave's recovery.

By the end of the second month, Julia would take Dave outside for short walks and as Dave hobbled along on his crutches, Julia helped to ensure he did not fall and cautioned him not to go beyond his ability. The nurse and her patient followed a path outside the hospital that the janitor had shoveled. Even though it was well below zero, Dave was thankful to get a few minutes of fresh air and to talk about almost everything with Nurse Burrs.

It was nearly six months after his first time up on crutches that the two were slowly ambling along quite far from the hospital. Dave's recovery had been amazing and as they walked with the sun shining and the birds singing in the trees, he needed to rest. They sat down on a bench in the shade of the large trees and for a long while, they just gazed out at the beautiful spring day.

"Now this is worth living for." Dave said. Julia agreed and glanced toward Dave who was now staring at her. As they gazed into each others eyes, it seemed as though a magnet pulled them closer together and the kiss was inevitable. They continued embracing for some time until Julia pulled back.

"Dave, I don't know what come over me. This is no way for a nurse to act with her patient," she said.

"Well, it's no way for a patient to act with his nurse either," he said feigning defensiveness. "Of course I know what come over us." He grinned as he continued to gaze into her eyes.

"What?" she asked anxiously.

"Love, Darlin', can't you hear the birds singing

our love song. They're doing it just for us." Julia listened and then a relaxed smile changed her face as her eyes moved toward the tree branches and then back to Dave's.

"Ahmm, well in that case," she whispered and she moved closer and they kissed and embraced with more fervor.

In the hospital, Dave was doing simple exercises and stretches to get motion back in his joints. This, combined with the daily walks with Julia, continued for several more weeks, but the day finally came that he was released from the hospital. After gathering his belongings and signing some papers, he sauntered over to the admitting area and hung around the desk until Julia came on shift. When she saw him standing there, she put two and two together and tears began to well up in her eyes.

"So I guess you'll be heading home to Prince Albert now?"

"Yeah, I'll go back to P.A. to recuperate some more and then I'll have to get a physical and see if I can pick up my training again. I don't even know if they'll let me back in." Now as they stared into each other's eyes, Julia's glossed over with tears.

"Will I ever see you again?" she asked.

"Well, uh." He cleared his throat. "Uh, that's what I've been waiting here for. I know we haven't known each other long, but I was wondering if you might consider, uh, becoming my, uh, wife?"

"You said you were going to try to continue your fighter pilot training?"

"Yeah, I think I might make it and then I'll do my bit for my country."

Julia thought for a long moment.

"Then I think I would rather wait until you get back from doing your bit for King and country, before I give you my answer. I'm sorry to say it, but I just don't think I could stand to marry you and then lose you." Now the tears were running down her cheeks.

Dave's countenance fell and he found it hard to speak. *How could I ever hold my head up if I didn't try to fulfill my obligation, but at the same time I can't go on without Julia.* Finally after a long silence he gently grasped her hands and again peered into her eyes.

"Honey, I have to re-join the training if possible and do my duty overseas. I could never feel right having others giving their life and limb for my freedom while I sat here in safety. I know you wouldn't want me that way either. Wouldn't it be better, if I were shot down, to at least have the memory of the short time we had together now?" He gazed at her searching for her answer and after a short moment he saw a hint of a smile on her face as she stared at her shoes.

"I guess I'll have to come to P.A. with you and meet your parents." Dave's face lit up.

"Then you'll marry me? You'll really marry me?"

Julia slowly nodded and Dave scooped her into

his arms and lifted her off the floor. Just then the Head Matron came up the hall and upon seeing the embrace and Dave kissing one of her nurses right in the foyer, she hurried over.

"Mister,, Lysik!" She exclaimed in a loud voice, drawing the Mr and Lysik out in disgust. "What in heaven's name do you think you're doing? And Miss Burrs, this is not a bordello you know." Dave quickly took a half step between the Matron and Julia.

"Now just a minute madam, that's no way to talk to my future wife," he said with as much sternness and authority as he could muster.

"You two are to be married? When on earth did that happen?"

"Dave just asked me and I said yes." Julia announced modestly. The older woman turned and threw up her hand in a sign of resignation as she walked away.

"You young people - you move too fast for me. Julia, I guess you'd better take a few weeks off, unless you plan on getting married in the hallway."

xxxxxxxxxxxxxxxxxxxxxxxxxxxxxxxxxxxxx

Dave stood at attention in front of Major Johnson who had already received the young man's medical report. The Major moved behind his desk.

"At ease, Aircraftsman Lysik" the Major ordered. "As far as I can see, with this doctor's report of your overall condition, you seem to have healed very quickly. I'm going to extend your sick leave by one month and at the end of that time, you'll be required to re-submit to a medical exam. If you qualify, you'll continue from where you left off."

"Aircraftsman Lysik would like to apologize for the accident, Sir." Dave said. Johnson held the palms of his hands out toward Dave.

"No, no, we checked it out son, and the accident wasn't your fault. You did everything by the book, but it seems there was some problem with the landing gear lock mechanism. Your record is clear, but I've got to say I don't want to have to hand out metals posthumously for air crashes in my training sector. Do I make myself clear?"

"Perfectly, Sir, but I've received something even better from the accident."

"I think you better explain yourself son."

"Well, I met this girl Sir."

"Speak up."

Dave cleared his throat.

"I met this girl, and we're engaged to be married. I was just wondering. Do you allow married men in the Service Flight Training School?"

"Son where the hell did you find time to date a girl and propose marriage? You were almost dead seven months ago and you've been in the hospital all this time." Dave was getting a little nervous, but still excited.

33

"She's a nurse Sir - the most beautiful girl I've ever met. See, she's right out there in the taxi." The major glanced out the window and then did a double-take. He cleared his throat as he returned his attention to the young recruit in front of him.

"Yes, I can see she is very pretty. Well there certainly isn't any regulation that hinders married men from going through the training and anyone who has gone through what you have and comes out of the hospital engaged to be married certainly has the right stuff. We'll see you back here on…" He checked the calendar on his desk. "August twenty-one, 07:00 - which gives you one month to make her your Purple Heart bride." The major now had a wide grin. "And Aircraftsman Lysik…"

"Yes Sir?"

"Congratulations."

"Yes Sir and thank you Sir." Dave slapped a sharp salute and left.

The Purple Heart Bride
Chapter 3

The drive north to Prince Albert was a long and sometimes treacherous one. Due to the fact that individual farmers contracted to maintain sections of the highway, Dave found some stretches to be quite smooth where he would speed up. Inevitably, though, he would come upon a poorly maintained piece of highway that required all his driving skill to keep the nearly new Chevrolet Coupe on the road. It was the spring of 1941 and with the combination of ruts, mud and the fact that Julia persisted in kissing him with alarming frequency, Dave had no choice but to pull to the shoulder of the road and stop the car. The two would wrap each other in their arms exchanging caresses and kisses that could have powered a steam generator.

Early in the evening, Dave worked the car down a muddy road, trying hard not to allow the wheels to slip into the deep ruts that a farm truck had formed. The only relief to the struggle was when he passed over a stretch of cord wood road where logs had been laid side by side across the road and then covered with gravel. He thought back to when his dad had worked on this stretch of road to make it passable over a bog. Soon Dave pointed to a large two-story farm house.

"That's our farm," he said pointing at the Lysik

family home. As they drove up the long driveway, Dave's father was the first to appear, down at the barn. The forty-year old man hurried up to the house and was almost to the car when Dave's mother stepped out onto the veranda. Both mother and father glowed with pride and excitement at seeing their boy again. Dave jumped out of the car and took the few quick steps to his father.

"Hi Dad," he said as he wrapped his arms around the man. Veronica moved quickly and was soon only a breath away. Dave turned and gave his mother a huge hug and kissed her cheek. At this moment, his mother's emotions brought her to tears. They were tears of thanksgiving, because her boy had come through his accident and was still alive. Dave turned to Julia with his hand out, beckoning her to move to his side.

"Mother, Father, this is Julia Burrs. As I wrote you, we intend to get married here before I get my medical next month for re-entry into flying school. Isn't she beautiful?" Dave glanced at Julia and noticing that she looked a bit embarrassed, nodded at his parents for confirmation. They both gave her a loving smile and then agreed while giving their future daughter-in-law a hug. The group then asked and answered questions as they gradually moved into the house. Once comfortable in the large living room, Mr. Lysik senior dropped the question.

"So what happens now?"

"I hope to get medical clearance and finish my training," Dave answered.

"And then I suppose you'll be assigned to a desk job?" Dave was taken by surprise by his father's comment, as the thought had never crossed his mind.

"Oh no, dad, I'm going to go right back and try to pick up where I left off. I'll get my hours in and then I'll be sent over to England." Neither Charles nor Veronica smiled now.

"Son, don't you think your accident was a sign from the Lord that maybe you should sit this one out?" Charles questioned in a no-nonsense way. Dave stared at his dad long and hard and came to the decision his father was just concerned for him.

"Not at all," Dave said. "In fact if the crash was a sign, I think it was that this war won't kill me and I can help stop that little thug in Germany from killing a lot of our people. Anyway, if they'll have me, I'll go." With the subject of their son's future discussed and apparently decided, Julia became the focal point.

"So will your parents be coming for the wedding?" Veronica asked. Julia blushed and Dave thought that he could see her eyes welling up.

"No, ah, no they won't be here," she managed to say. She glanced at Dave. "My mother was killed in a car accident and my father was so distraught he committed suicide. It was only a couple of years ago." Her eyes welled up. Victoria had some tears already, but came to the rescue.

"Well with such a fine young lady for a daughter I'm sure they'd have been here if they could. Charles, you'll have to act as the bride's father and give her away," Veronica said as she wiped her eyes with a handkerchief. "Oh Lord, I don't know how I'll manage to get through the ceremony. I guess I had better be well-stocked with these."

"I swear mother, you'd cry if someone just played the wedding march, without a wedding," Charles said, light-heartedly. Veronica was getting close to tears again, so she made a gesture to Julia and the two ladies went to the kitchen to fix some coffee and a snack. Charles had just returned to the original subject of Dave holding back from going back to fighter training when Ezekiel, Dave's youngest brother burst into the living room.

"Hey little brother! Heard you cracked up one of McKenzie's expensive planes. How long you gonna be in the slammer for?" Zeke said as he laughed at his own joke. By now Dave was off the couch and trying to get his younger brother in a headlock.

"Call me little brother will you." He looked around at his dad who had cleared his throat and was frowning. "What do you do with this twerp, stretch him every night? He just keeps getting taller."

"OK, you two settle down while you're in the house. Next thing you know you'll break some of mother's new china." Charles nodded to the shelves on the wall that were adorned with a full complement of expensive china. Dave had never seen the china before, so he gave Zeke a shove and walked over to gaze at the collection. It was some time before he whistled and said, "That must have set you back a pretty penny." Dave turned and chuckled, "I suppose that means no tossing the football in the house?"

"And no more rough-housing in the house either," Charles added.

"I think I've missed hearing that for the last year," Dave said with a chuckle, but it was true. He really had missed home and the love of his family.

xxxxxxxxxxxxxxxxxxxxxxxxxxxxxxxxxxxxxxxxxx

As Dave gazed around the small church, he felt like a very nervous king whose queen would soon be escorted down the aisle to him. His family was Jewish but had converted to Presbyterian and Charles had become a deacon at the little church. Dave felt well-dressed in his new blue RCAF dress uniform and he suspected that Julia would be even more radiant than usual.

I wonder if I should pinch myself to prove this is all real, Dave thought. As if the magic of the moment caused it, the piano began the wedding march and when Dave turned to watch the procession, his eyes fell on his bride who was more beautiful than he ever imagined. Charles, projecting such a proud demeanor that could have easily been mistaken for Julia's own parent, escorted her to her husband-to-be and then turned to sit down beside an already sobbing Veronica. The music went silent.

"*Dearly beloved, we are gathered here to witness this couple being joined in Holy matrimony. We remind them that they are performing an act of complete faith, each in the other - that the heart of their marriage will be the relationship created in heaven, but that they must nurture. This marriage is an act of faith similar to the faith in Jesus that is to salvation. In a world where faith often falls short of expectation, it is a tribute to these two who now join hands and hearts in perfect faith and love. If there be any here who believe that there is reason why these two should not be joined, let them come forward now or forever hold their peace.*" The preacher stopped and scanned the full church, wishing Sunday service could be this well attended. He then turned back to the couple.

"*Do you, Dave Matthew Lysik, take Julia Evelyn Burrs to be your lawfully wedded wife? Do you promise to love, honor, cherish and protect her, forsaking all others and holding only to her?*"

"I do," Dave said, without hesitation. The preacher continued.

"Do you, Julia Evelyn Burrs, take Dave Matthew Lysik to be your lawfully wedded husband? Do you promise to love, honor, cherish and protect him, forsaking all others and holding only unto him?" Julia turned and gazed into Dave's eyes for several moments with a love deeper than the ocean, before she answered.

"I do," she said.

Dave turned and took a ring from George.

"With this ring, I thee wed; all my love, I give you," he said, as he clumsily placed the ring on her finger. Julia also received a ring from one of her bridesmaids, then turned to Dave and repeated the same vow, placing the ring on his finger.

Dave glanced around at his parents and saw that his mother was sniffling, but noticed that his dad's eyes were glassy as well. A lump formed in his throat. He was the proudest man in the universe, or at least he thought so.

The preacher cleared his own throat and proceeded.

"It is my honour then by the office of Bishop under God to pronounce you man and wife. What God has brought together, let no man try to separate." He smiled at the two happy young people in front of him. *"Dave, you may kiss your bride."*

Dave hesitated too long, so Julia grabbed his neck and pulled their lips together to kiss him long and hard, to the clapping, hooting and whistling of those in the church. Later, as they left the church, Julia flung her bridal bouquet and noticed that a young girl had caught it. At that moment, the two of them were instantly showered with confetti and rice and Dave noticed the string of tin cans tied to the bumper of the Chevrolet with "just married" elaborately painted on the trunk.

Dave was happy to see George Waters at the reception and talked with him briefly. George informed him of how he had washed out at Mossbank as a pilot and had been transferred to eastern Canada. He said that he had been reassigned as a navigator and he was sure that he would be stepping off very soon. Both men were saddened by this, because they had both hoped to be together and fly Hurricanes or Spitfires. As the evening wore on, the reception took on a more festive nature, with most of the men and some of the women becoming more inebriated. Dave and Julia said their quick goodbyes and left. They would spend their first night as newlyweds at the farm and then honeymoon for two weeks in Saskatoon in a rented apartment. Dave would then need to report back for his medical after which they would return to Weyburn. Early the next morning, they hugged and said goodbye to their parents, and John, George and Zeke. Dave retraced their drive back through Prince Albert and then to Saskatoon. Julia was slightly more subdued when it came to necking with Dave while he was driving, but he still had to pull over numerous times for passionate respites.

Xxxxxxxxxxxxxxxxxxxxxxxxxxxxxxxxxxxxxxxxxxx

The newly-wedded couple found the apartment and after Dave carried Julia across the threshold, he gazed around.

"I think this place must have been built before the last war," Dave said with a chuckle.

"I think its romantic," Julia said. "Besides it looks like it's just been remodeled and it's got all the necessities." Julia scanned the room. "And look here, the landlord has even placed a bouquet of roses on the table with a note." Dave picked up the card.

"It says, please accept my congratulations… and enjoy the bottle of French wine in the refrigerator. Love, George Waters. The landlord had provisioned the pantry at Dave's request and laid out fresh linens.

The newly-weds fixed a quick snack and sipped some wine while conversing mostly about the wedding, but soon lovemaking became an overwhelming desire and they melted into an embrace.

For the next two weeks, they spent many afternoons walking around Saskatoon, enjoying sodas, just talking and of course, enjoying intimate pleasures. Too soon, it was the day Dave felt revulsion for - the day he must qualify with a new medical.

The doctor was very thorough and especially tested joint movement and reaction. Finally, he finished and asked Dave to wait in his office while he finished up with another patient. Dave waited in anticipation for the doctor to return and tell him he had passed. The doctor slowly entered the room, closed the door and slowly sat down behind a desk stacked with several reference books from the volumes along the wall. The physician lit a cigarette as he peered at his patient.

"I hope you understand that the government pays me to be absolutely impartial and thorough, so I'll tell it like I'll report it to them. First, I've got to say that your healing has been, well, almost a miracle. I would have never believed that anyone with the amount of injuries you had when you were brought into the hospital in Weyburn, would have progressed so far so soon." He stopped there to let what he had said sink in. A smile began to spread on Dave's face. He was sure that he would get a pass now.

"And although you have healed exceptionally, you have lost some movement in your knees and ankles - maybe five percent. Nothing to be concerned about though," he added quickly. "There is, however, a small loss of neurological motor ability that will definitely work as a negative when it comes to the physical requirements necessary to pass as a fighter pilot. I am therefore unable to pass you in this physical." The smile had long since left Dave's lips and a sad, worried demeanor took its place.

"You mean I can't fly anymore?" The doctor answered quickly.

"Oh, you might pass the medical for slower planes, maybe bombers or transport, but not fighters."

"Will it get better so I might in the future?" The doctor shook his head.

"Barring an out-and-out miracle, I would say no, but who can tell. In a year or two, maybe," the doctor said, without showing any optimism. Dave contemplated for a moment.

"How about heavier, slower planes, like bombers, could you pass my physical for flying one of them?" Dave was trying to squeeze a last concession from the doc.

"Given the specifications the government stipulates for multi-engine aircraft, such as bombers, you would probably pass that with flying colors. If you like, I would be happy to note that in my report. Of course, your C.O. would have the last word on that. So far as my paperwork is concerned at this point though, you cannot pass the physical for a fighter pilot."

Dave thanked the doctor and agreed for him to insert the note that he was capable for multi-engine or smaller slower aircraft. He left the doctor's office and spent the day wandering around the park and then the city. He was devastated. He considered flying the bombers for a while until recovered and then slip into a fighter squadron. Flying a spit was what he had always wanted to do ever since he seen a picture of one in a magazine in the hardware store and he certainly wasn't impressed with the idea of flying any of those huge sluggish monsters for the rest of his time. The problem was now, that was the only option open to him, if he could even get approval for that. His mind went around in a circle and wound up at the beginning - trying to decide whether he even wanted to fly the big ones at all. He mulled it over and just couldn't seem to get his mind around it. The sun was going down when he finally returned home.

"Where have you been for so long, honey," Julia crooned. At that, Dave jumped into the sofa and threw a pillow to the other end. He brooded a while as Julia stood waiting for a reply. Finally, he grabbed the pillow again, while glaring into her eyes.

"I didn't pass the medical," he said in a broken voice. Julia instantly sat down beside him.

"What was wrong? You seemed to have healed very well."

"The doctor says my reactions are too slow. He has recommended I ask for training in larger, slower aircraft, like Wellingtons, Halifaxs or transports. I don't want to fly them," he said with an agonized voice. Julia leaned over and kissed him tenderly on the cheek.

"I thought those huge monsters were going to do a lot to win the war. Wasn't it Churchill who said 'the fighters will give us salvation, but the bombers will give us victory'?"

"Ah what the hell does he know? He's just another politician," Dave said angrily. Julia stood up and faced her husband.

"You take that back, David Lysik! Mr. Churchill is more than just a politician. He's a statesman and I believe he will help lead the Allies to victory. He's managed to hold back the Germans so far. Seems to me that's what you said you wanted to do and now because you can't fly..." she flitted her hands in the air until she remembered the phrase, "fighter planes, you're upset. Do you want to do your part in the war or don't you?" Dave had never heard Julia talk like that before, and he was taken aback, but it had the effect she wanted. He sat there, contemplating what she had said for a long while and then noticed her raising her eyebrows in a way that physically requested a response. He shrugged in resignation.

"You're right on all fronts. The man surely had his hands full just trying to stop the Hun and overrule or manipulate his own parliament at the same time. Hell, even Roosevelt can't manage that. And yes, I still do want to do my part, but I got to tell you I really had my heart set on flying a Spit." His demeanor relaxed as he pulled her down on top of himself and as she giggled, he kissed and caressed her. After a long interlude of lovemaking, they lay on the couch, softly conversing. Dave was smiling.

"Hey, I just remembered. I forgot to tell you, but George was reassigned as a navigator. Said he washed out at Mossbank - he didn't say why. I wonder if we'll cross paths."

"I would think that could be very possible. After all, you're both fighting on the same side." Julia said, snickering. Dave was feeling better now that his mind had been relieved of its conflict.

"Hey, honey, how about a date?" Dave asked unexpectedly.

"What do you mean - how about a date? We're married, remember?" she said sarcastically. They were both standing in the living room.

"Doesn't mean a fella can't ask his best girl out for dinner and dancing does it? What do you say?" By now, he was behind her and with a hand on her shoulder, he turned her around and gave her another passionate kiss.

"Well," she said, almost singing, "Seeing you put it that way, lead on McDuff."

They dined at a small, quiet restaurant where Dave ordered a bottle of champagne for starters. They both ordered the roast duck dinner and spent a leisurely couple of hours. Dave then took his new wife to the dance hall and they danced into the wee hours. They laughed and talked and when they finally entered the apartment, they faced each other.

"I had a great time tonight Honey," Dave said.

"Well so did I, but the night's not over yet." She eyed the bedroom and Dave's mouth curled up in a grin.

The young couple were still sleeping the next morning when a knock on the door woke them up. Dave stumbled out of bed, stubbed his toe on a chair leg and partly hopped on one foot to the door. He opened the door to find a young boy standing there. The boy held out a telegram and asked for Dave Lysik. Dave acknowledged, signed and thanked the boy. As Dave closed the door, Julia asked who it was. Dave opened the envelope.

"It's a telegram," he said, as he began reading. "Whoa, it says I'm to report to Mossbank Commanding Officer's office at 0500 hours tomorrow. Julia appeared from the bedroom with a smile, but the tears in her eyes betrayed her attempt to show courage. When Dave noticed, he rushed over to her and held her for a long while.

The Purple Heart Bride
Chapter 4

Dave stood at attention in the base Commander's office until he was given his ease.

"Son, I received your medical and I'm sad to say you washed out. I'll need to find an alternate slot for you. Maybe gunnery or navigator, but you're definitely out of fighters." Dave had a hard time making his voice audible.

"Sir, I don't want to sound disrespectful, but the doctor said I would still pass the physical for larger or slower aircraft. It was just the fighters he didn't pass me on. Would it be possible to transfer training to multiple engines?" The Wing Commander studied the doctor's report closer.

"Hmm, I see what you mean." The CO's face lightened with a smile. "Yes I think that is exactly the way we should proceed." He searched Dave's face. "Have the lieutenant there issue the appropriate papers and we'll see if we can't get you back in the air. There was a moment's silence and then the CO glanced at Dave who was momentarily stunned by the sudden and unusual swiftness of military progress. "Dismissed."

"Yes Sir," Dave said giving a snappy salute. He turned to leave and the commander went back to his paperwork, but then decided to add a little locker room pep talk.

"Lysik!"

"Yes Sir?" Dave swung around.

"You be ready for the most intensive training in your life."

"Yes Sir."

The next morning Dave was reinstated in the S.F.T.S. and immediately began with subjects in the classroom. He spent days learning about the multi-engine planes he would be trained on. He had to learn every mechanism possible on the Avro Anson and then the instruction melded into flight training. One day blurred into another as the intensified training took place in whirlwind fashion. Dave was determined to get back in the air and his marks on the test papers showed his determination.

It was June 30, 1941, and the day had finally come for his first solo flight as pilot since the accident. It would be in the Anson. Dave scanned the sky for any sign of a storm, but saw only some small, white cumulus clouds very slowly moving across the sky. "*A perfect day for flying,*" he told himself. He followed his flight examiner, a lieutenant, out to the aircraft. Dave stepped into the plane and made his way to the pilot's seat. He could see that the Anson was a carpenter's dream. It surely wasn't designed for battle like the Bolingbrock, but it was great for twin engine training. Dave settled in and gazed at the instruments panel. He studied each gauge and switch as his instructor went through a pre-flight check and explained the gauges and equipment found in the Anson, even though Dave could recite it from memory. The gear was no longer complicated to him and the lieutenant gave him the nod to taxi out. It was time for his first take-off since the crash and he was well aware that the officer beside him in the jump seat was watching for his reactions and ready to take control of the plane if he faltered. He relayed the pre-flight check to the officer as he realized that a large part of his subconscious mind had been astir with emotions and now he realized that it had little to do with flying fighters. What he thought was his desire to be able to fly a Spitfire was more that he needed to prove to himself that he wasn't afraid of getting back in an aircraft and piloting it back into the air. He shivered when he thought of landing it.

He finished the check and then, as ordered, taxied out to the end of runway three-six. He moved flaps to ten percent and waited for the signal to take off. When the blue flare arced into the sky, he spooled up the engines. As they reached their speed, he released the brake and raised the throttles. The plane picked up speed quickly as the aircraft creaked and rumbled down the runway. He moved the throttles to one hundred percent and within a couple of seconds, the plane defied gravity and suddenly smoothed out as if it was sitting in a cloud.

Dave zeroed the flaps and retracted the landing gear. The Anson slowly picked up speed and altitude. When they reached the required five thousand feet and Dave had throttled back to cruising speed, the officer ordered a left ninety-degree bank coming to a heading of two one zero degrees. The instructor had no sooner uttered the last syllable than Dave banked the plane and came to the required heading. They flew on, with the instructor allowing him to fly for a prescribed amount of time and then having him turn to one two zero degrees, then after another amount of time, ordering another ninety degree turn to zero three zero degrees. The instructor waited until they were almost perpendicular to runway three-six and then ordered yet another ninety to bring the craft around to a heading of two nine eight degrees. During the last two headings Dave had lost fifteen hundred feet and was now in perfect position for the landing. He lowered the landing gear and set full flaps and increased power to eighty percent. The Anson responded sluggishly, but accurately and as the tires touched the pavement there was a slight screech and jolt. The aircraft quickly slowed with the tail wheel settling to pavement. Dave applied more brakes and the plane came to a stop. They had flown a perfect rectangle and landed perfectly. The apprehension from his previous crash had certainly dissipated and Dave had a wide grin as the instructor informed him that all he required now was flying hours. Dave knew that everything was going to work out just fine.

Once he passed exams with the Anson, he learned the same on the Bolingbroke. The Bolly, as it was referred to, was considerably larger than the Anson, but it was a smaller bomber, as bombers go, than the Halifax. Never-the-less, it packed a significant punch for its size. It was a twin-engine plane with the capability to carry a heavy load.

Several weeks later, Dave stood on the tarmac beside a Bolly he had just landed and watched as a much larger plane landed. As he watched it land, a corporal stepped up.

"Aircraftman David Lysik?"

"Yes?" Dave replied.

"The wing commander would like to see you in his office." Dave glanced back at the aircraft that had just landed. "Immediately Sir," the corporal added purposefully, regaining Dave's full attention. Dave nodded and proceeded directly to the commander's office.

Dave entered the office and immediately came to attention with a snappy salute.

"At ease, Pilot Officer." Dave jerked his eyes toward the man, hearing the term and thinking that there must be some mistake. The officer glanced up at Dave with a grin.

"You heard right, Pilot Officer Lysik." He moved around his desk and produced a pendant of wings and a patch for his uniform. "I'm sorry we can't perform this on parade, but the clock is ticking." After shaking hands and congratulating Dave, he moved back behind his desk and shuffled some papers. Once he found the file, he wanted, the wing commander looked up and shot Dave a smile. "Mr. Lysik, I suppose you saw the Lancaster that just flew in." He waited for Dave to reply.

"The large four-engine plane? Yes sir."

"Well, I have a request to assign one of our best trainees to fly with the lieutenant colonel for the next short while and your name seems to top the list. What do you think? Figure you could learn a few things in that cockpit?" his commanding officer asked, his grin widening as he saw the excitement in the young man's eyes.

"Ahh, yes Sir. That would be great," Dave said, getting more excited by the second.

"Alright, then it's done. You will report to Lieutenant Colonel Roberts tomorrow at 0600. Oh, and if you would like to meet him beforehand, it's said he'll be at the Hostess club tonight. And Lysik, get those patches and wings sewn on."

"Yes Sir. Thank you Sir." The wing commander dismissed him and Dave left, still wondering if he were dreaming.

The Hostess club was a Mason's Lodge building in the town of Mossbank. Dave went, but couldn't find the Colonel anywhere and finally headed back to barracks. He found it hard to sleep due to the excitement of his new orders and the next morning he was waiting beside the Lancaster until Colonel Roberts arrived.

For the next few weeks Dave flew with the colonel and learned the eccentricities of the Lancaster. Sometimes Dave thought that Roberts mistook the large bomber for a fighter. He made the big plane do things Dave would have sworn it couldn't do. He showed him how to slow the plane down, seemingly sitting in mid-air to almost stall speed, with the flaps full down and then speed up again. The pilot showed him how to evade and corkscrew. Dave absorbed the information like a sponge, learning what some pilots never learn in a lifetime. And so it was with a bittersweet feeling that he watched the large plane finally lift off and fly away without him. The aircraft was heading for Victory Aircraft Factory in Malton Ontario where the engineers would literally take the big plane apart to study so that Canada could begin building the Lancaster with Canadian gauges and equipment.

xxxxxxxxxxxxxxxxxxxxxxxxxxxxxxxxxxxxxxxxx

It was after only one week back at piloting the Bolingbroke that Dave received his orders to transfer to RCAF Base Dartmouth in Nova Scotia. He had one week of leave and then would fly a nearly new Bolingbroke to Nova Scotia, where he would be given further orders. Although Dave didn't believe that this was his big step-off, he never-the-less felt a strange knot in his gut. He wasn't really fearful, but he knew that he might not see Julia for a very long time. He booked off on leave with his mind made up; Julia and he would have a good time before he left.

He arrived at their apartment and Dave's first course of action was to sweep Julia into his arms. They remained in an embrace for several minutes. By the time they separated, Dave could see the tears welling up in Julia's eyes. He stared into her blue eyes.

"I've been ordered to Nova Scotia. I'll be flying a bomber there, but as far as I know I'll be stationed there. If I am, I'll send for you and we can live off of the base." He pulled her close for another embrace.

"When do you have to go?" she asked, almost dreading the answer.

"I have seven days' leave and I thought if you were agreed we could head up to the farm and visit my folks." Julia put on her best brave face.

"I think that would be a great idea. I would really like to see them again."

XXXXXXXXXXXXXXXXXXXXXXXXXXXXXXXXXXXXXXXX

The trip was hot and dusty as the June 1941 heat wave enveloped the prairies. As they drove north of Prince Albert, Dave watched several farmers out in their fields stooking some oats for green feed. Shortly thereafter, he caught sight of the rotating paddles of a binder moving across the field of oats. It was cutting the grain, producing sheaves and depositing them in piles at nearly equal intervals. Surveying the scene suddenly evoked memories of when his dad had taught him to stook. He remembered how the muscular man had grabbed four sheaves, two in each hand, holding them near the twine with a good handful of the straw.

"You take the sheaves like this," his father had said as he held them in the air and then firmly smacked the butt end of the straw on the ground, leaning them together. "Then just build another four or six leaning onto those." He quickly accomplished exactly what he described and when he had finished, it had the appearance of a miniature straw hut. "If the crop is heavy, you can have up to ten or twelve sheaves to a stook. You probably want to start with just one sheaf in each hand." He stepped back and motioned for Dave to give it a try. "Just so long as the air can get in but most of the rain can't," he added. Dave had followed his dad's instruction and by the end of the day the field was covered with the rounded rectangle stacks of sheaves that gave the appearance of a large town of miniature straw huts. Dave imagined it looked like a Middle Ages farming town. Dave remembered at the end of the day, as he climbed into bed, it wasn't long before his eyes grew heavy and he fell into a restful sleep. Even as he thought back on that first day of stooking, he grimaced. As his memory ventured still further, he then smiled as he remembered that the next days were still hard work, but he had become more accustomed to it. Julia, sitting beside him in the car, had been watching him.

"I'd say from the look on your face that you miss the farm," she said. It brought Dave out of his reverie.

"I certainly have some good memories. There is nothing like the harvest and the feeling of accomplishment and expectation. You work hard all year and if everything goes right and you have a good harvest you get to live good for another year with food and other needs. Possibly buy a new implement or something for the house. Trouble is, the last long while, things haven't gone all that well. The dry conditions and the depression have put many farmers off the land and into the unemployment lines." Julia gazed at him.

"But your family seems to have made it pretty well."

"Oh things were tight for a long while, but up north, I guess you could say we were a little closer to the bone anyway. We didn't have the big acreage spreads they had down south so even in the good times we didn't have the crops they had and when the drought years hit, we didn't have as much to lose. Also, we were closer to the forests and everything it has to offer, so we got by." Julia gazed at her man, admiring him with a love that was deeper than the ocean. She knew it was mutual.

The time went by much too quickly, with Dave helping his dad and brother in the field and Julia helping her mother-in-law in the kitchen. Even though they were all working hard, they found time to visit and when the time ran out, it was a sad departure. The drive back to Regina was very much more morose than the trip north. If the drive had been quiet, it was only a reflection of their feelings by the time they arrived home. Dave didn't feel this was the way to spend his last evening and night with Julia, so he tried to insert some light.

"Honey, I think we should get dinner at one of those fancy hotel restaurants and then go to the officers' club for dancing," he said, grabbing her and pretending to do the lead up to the jitter-bug.

"I think the dinner is OK, but how about us coming back here. I think I just want you all to myself tonight." Dave realized that her idea was way better all the way around and agreed. And so it was that the night before he was to go to war, they enjoyed an elegant meal and made passionate love late into the evening.

Dave awoke Julia from her fitful sleep at three in the morning and they made the drive to Mossbank. The trip was crammed with promises to write every day, plans for Julia to move when Dave knew he was staying, tears and silence.

The silent parts where the worst. The car was barely moving up the gravelled road to the airbase and just after they passed the checkpoint at the perimeter, they could see the Bolingbroke sitting in front of the bunker. As the Chevrolet stopped, Julia grabbed Dave in a hug and their kiss was long and hard. Tears were streaming down her face as her mind conjured up a much more ominous fate for her lover than reality. Finally, they sat for a moment and then Dave went to get out of the car. Julia grabbed him and hugged him one more time and began to slide over to get out the driver's side as well.

"Honey, stay in the car. I'm not sure I'll be able to leave if I can see you outside," he said with his own eyes filling with tears. He gave her a last kiss, grabbed his duffel bag out of the back seat and hurried off to the plane. The Bolly was fueled and ready. He climbed in the hatch, stuffed his duffel bag in the back and with orders to report to Wing Commander Dupont at Shearwater upon arrival and his flight plan laid out, took off down the runway, lifting off from the Saskatchewan training base at 0530 September 25, 1941. Julia watched through her tears until the plane was out of sight. It was all she could do, with the tears streaming down her face, to keep the Chevy on the road back to Weyburn.

The flying weather was great and the large two-engine bomber made its noisy way through the skies as it headed for the east coast. Dave had one stop en-route and barely enough fuel to make it. It got harrowing just before he got to the port of call, as the fuel gauge was nearing the empty mark. Wondering if he had somehow missed the airport, he believed he was flying on fumes by the time he saw the runway.

He found the ground crew at the airfield very hospitable and they took him to the mess hall, showed him to a barracks and a bed that had been allocated. He slept well and the next morning after a great breakfast he lifted off, just as the sun came over the horizon. It was a non-eventful flight and he caught sight of the east-west strip to the Dartmouth airbase, just as he was losing the light of the sun behind him.

The Purple Heart Bride
Chapter 5

Dave was directed to a barracks and given a billet. He was told that the wing commander expected him in his office at 0:600 and left to get some sleep. It was nearly midnight before Dave finally slipped into a fitful sleep. He was awakened by a corporal at 0:530 and he hurried to shower and get ready for his meeting. The administration offices were not easily identified and sadly, no one had given him proper directions. It was just after 0:615 that a lieutenant showed him into the wing commander's office where he was told that the commander would join him shortly. Dave worried that he would be reprimanded for tardiness and thought he might lose his last promotion; as time went on that worry became less and boredom began to set in. After a two-hour wait, the officer entered as if a whirlwind was chasing him and quickly moved behind his desk.

"You'll have to excuse me, but we are fairly busy around here." He shuffled some papers on his desk and then stopped, seeming to notice Dave for the first time. "I'm sorry - I'm Wing Commander Gilles Dupont and we really are pushed to the limit out here." Again he shuffled some papers, although this time Dave got the impression that he was looking for something.

Finally, he pulled out a manila folder with a sheaf of papers inside.

"Ah, here we are. These are your orders. Seems you're to exchange dust in your eyes for webbed toes for a few weeks. You will be stationed here until you are scheduled on a ship, at which time you will report to Halifax harbor. I hear the wait for a troupe carrier is normally about a month. You will commence duties by co-piloting a B-24 Liberator and patrolling for German U-boats until embarkation. Are there any questions?" Dave took the papers offered him and began to read his orders. He stopped abruptly.

"Sir, these orders have my rank wrong," he said as he pointed to them with his finger. "I just got promoted to Flight Officer and they keep referring to me in here as Flight Lieutenant." As he spoke, he glanced up and noticed a grin come across the wing commander's face.

"Congratulations, Flight Lieutenant Lysik, you just got one of those unexplained promotions that no one ever understands or wants to try and explain," he said, as he offered Dave a set of the standard-sized twin stripes and shook his hand. "I hear it has something to do with the war and a certain training mission in an experimental Lancaster. Your liberator is similar in size and lift. Young man, you're one of the few Canadians who have flown a four-engine of that size. You're dismissed and good hunting, Lieutenant." Dave

66

was speechless, but slapped a snappy salute.

"Thank you Sir."

Dave got back to the barracks just in time to meet the crew of the B-24 coming in from breakfast. Dave could see that the pilot was an older man - close to thirty and the eight other crew members were all older than Dave. He stood by his bunk and felt somewhat out of place.

"I'm Flight Lieutenant Peter Wayne," the pilot said, as he threw out his hand. "I fly the bird while these guys throw rocks and the occasional depth charge at the U-boats." Peter smiled and Dave felt instant warmth radiate from this man's personality.

"David Lysik - I was just promoted to Flight Lieutenant and ordered to become your co-pilot." By now the others had gathered around.

"Well, we're glad you're here, Dave, because Carl - our regular co-pilot - came down with acute appendicitis. The doc says he'll be out of action for at least a month and maybe more. I'm Tony, the engineer and this tall fellow is our navigator. Tony pulled the tall guy forward. This is Andy and he really does tell us where to go and how to get there." Dave laughed with the group as he shook Andy's hand. At that instant, the introductions were interrupted by a corporal entering the barracks.

He stepped up to Peter and passed him a brown envelope.

"Your orders Sir," he said almost regretfully.

Peter opened the envelope and read. The smile left his face.

"Seems the folks in planning are getting nervous about the proximity of the U-boats again. We've been issued new orders," he said and folded the paper while raising his eyebrows in a defeated attitude. "All leaves are cancelled until further notice. Be ready to rotate in one hour." He turned to Dave.

"Well at least you won't get bored sitting around the barracks. Are you going to be all right without a briefing on the plane?"

"I think I should be in good shape. I read up on the B-17. It's a good plane unless someone is shooting at it."

"Yeah, it doesn't take well to being shot at and some of the subs do get in a few." He nodded at Dave's trunk. "Dress warm," he said and turned away to his own bunk.

Dave was awestruck as they flew ever farther over the Atlantic. Gazing down, he saw the endless waves with their white crowns frothing to a head and then disappearing, only to show up in a slightly different location. Hour after hour, he scanned the wide ocean as everyone else on the plane was doing.

"Have you ever come across any subs out here?" Dave asked.

"Oh, you bet, but we've only attacked two and I think we did some damage to one of them. The problem is they usually dive when they see us and by the time we get there, well, they're out of our reach. The destroyers can follow them with sonar but we don't have that so we have to try and surprise them," Peter said as he banked the large bomber for a 90 degree turn.

"Our best scenario is to see a periscope breaking the water and get them before they go down." Peter added. Dave thought about it for a while.

"Seems like a heck of a waste of money and time," Dave said

"I don't know about that, but once in a while we get lucky. The boys from Gander and the ones from Ireland have sunk nearly ten and that's helping get the supplies through to Britain where they're needed."

Dave went silent and continued watching for the telltale white v of the periscope. It was 30 minutes before Peter banked the plane again and they began their homeward leg and four hours later, they saw the aerodrome come into sight.

The crew secured their stations as Peter and Dave shut the plane down. Almost as one the crew filed out of the craft. Dave noticed that no one was speaking and neither was he. They had been in the B-24 9 hours and none of them had been to bed for close to twenty. He was so dog-tired, all he wanted to do was sleep. He slogged into the barracks, crashed onto his bunk and without getting undressed, fell into a deep sleep.

For the next five days they performed the same

ritual. Up at 0:600, breakfast at 0:630, in flight by 0:800, recon for nine hours, shower and dinner at 18:00 hours and hit the sack by 20:00.

To say Dave was getting bored with the routine would be to understate the situation. As he scanned the sea he wondered if he would ever get over to Britain where he knew the action really was. Suddenly, the voice of Paul, the front gunner crackled on the earphones.

"Periscope at two o'clock about ten miles. Heading straight for us." Dave snapped to the directions given and eventually saw the tiny wake of the protruding spy glass.

"Okay men, this is it. I think we might drop a depth charge on this one and sink her," Peter said. He had no sooner spoken, than he watched the submarine begin to surface. "Oh, oh, looks like she's coming up. Bombardier, be ready to drop a couple 100-pounders on that tub," he said and then turned to Dave. "This is where we earn our money. I think this one is going to try to fight as soon as she finds out we're here." Peter had already nosed the big bomber on a downhill slope and was picking up speed.

Sadly, the crew of the U-boat were very well trained and were at battle stations before Peter could get the B-24 over the sub. Its shells were coming fast. Paul was spraying the deck with his Brownings, but the submarine gunner managed to put a single 105 mm through the front turret and it continued through the windscreen on

Peter's side. Instantly, the plane had no front gunner and no pilot.

Dave grabbed the yoke and thereby control of the plane. Immediately, he revved all four engines, pulled back on the wheel and banked right, narrowly avoiding another shell which for the B-24 would likely have been a kill shot.

Those boys are hot, he thought.

The speed that was built up allowed Dave to squirm, one way and the other, banking hard to avoid the shells. When they were finally out of range, Dave glanced over at the mangled body of the pilot. There was no question of whether he was dead. Dave almost threw up. The top half of Peter's body was gone.

"OK, one at a time, I want damage reports starting with the rear turret," he said with as much authority as he could muster. It was better than he envisioned, but worse than he would like. The nose cone where the front gunner was stationed was completely gone, along with the left side windshield and side window. Most of the controls from the pilot's side were broken or just gone. Those on Dave's side, though, were all there and seemed to be working. Apparently there was a hole in the fuselage back from the wings, but it didn't seem to affect the plane. Luckily, it had missed the bombs and depth charges. Dave was now circling out of range of the sub trying to decide what to do. Of course, returning to base was what he had to do. He, however, didn't like the fact that the enemy had just killed a very good man. He weighed his options and decided to try one more time to sink the U-boat. Dave commanded the crew general quarters, battle stations and told the Bombardier to prepare two bombs. He lined up a bombing run and as the B-24 headed for the submarine, the German Captain ordered a dive.

"Bombardier, you got those two bombs ready?" Dave ordered on the intercom.

"Yes sir."

"Okay, when you're ready, take the plane and drop those suckers. If we get a hit, fine, if we don't, they'll probably submerge. You be ready with depth charges."

"Yes sir, how's the captain doing, sir," the bombardier asked. There was a long silence.

"Sorry… he didn't make it." There was silence and everyone left, came to a halt. Dave sensed the halt.

"Bombardier? Step to it! And the rest of you, I know how close you were to Lieutenant Wayne, so we need to do this for him. Now, let's get to it."

Dave manoeuvred the bomber to near the drop zone and the bombardier took over. Neither bomb hit, but they came very close and had the secondary effect Dave had mentioned. Dave banked hard and at the same time put the B-24 into a steep dive. The sub was under the water as the bomber screamed over the conning tower. Paul managed to dispense three depth charges as Dave pulled up and banked to get a view of what damage, if any, there was. As Dave and the crew scanned the area where the sub had been, there was a black oil slick and there was a great deal of flotsam. The third depth charge exploded as they watched and pushed the stern half of the sub to the surface. It had been ripped in half and as Dave circled, they saw that there were no survivors. It was time to go home.

There was yet another important decision to be made and that was which air base would be better: Gander or Shearwater. Gander was closer and should anything suddenly go wrong, there was more chance to get there. Dave checked the gauges and the rest of the plane and decided on Shearwater. The navigator gave him the heading and he set course for Nova Scotia.

By the time Dave got the Liberator shut down, the fire department was surrounding the plane. He had already radioed that the damage was severe with two casualties and that the aircraft was mechanically sound, but they came out anyway. Dave took a final glance at what was left of Peter and hurried out of the plane.

He hurried over to the edge of the tarmac, managed to kneel on one knee and then he vomited until there was nothing left on his stomach. When he tried to stand up, a corporal helped him to his feet.

"Sir," the corporal said, his eyes fixed on the blood covering Dave's left shoulder and side of his head. "The commander would like to see you in his office…" He stared again at the blood, "As soon as your wounds are taken care of and you're cleaned up… Are you alright, Sir?"

"I think I'll live, Corporal. At the moment I'm not really sure," Dave said, as he scratched his voice and spit, trying to clear his mouth of the awful taste. He ran his hand by the blood.

"This isn't my blood, it was the captain's," Dave said and nodded to the plane. He started feeling ill again, so he focused on the jeep that the man in front of him had arrived in. "Can you give us a ride to the barracks?"

"Oh, yes sir," the corporal said. Dave waved the crew over and they all piled on the small vehicle.

xxxxxxxxxxxxxxxxxxxxxxxxxxxxxxxxxxxxx

"Lieutenant Lysik, that was an outstanding kill out there. I guess I'm wondering why you didn't choose to break off and get you, your men and the extensively damaged plane back to base. I am assuming you will enlighten us as to how you made the decision to attack instead of break off … in your report… Whatever your reasons, it will probably get you and your crew some medals." The wing commander sat with raised eyebrows, waiting for a reply.

"Sir, my first thought was to insure the integrity of the aircraft. Once I understood its flying ability was not greatly compromised, I decided to proceed with an attack on the U-boat. It was also in my mind to get retribution for Lieutenant Wayne and our front gunner," Dave said.

Dupont gazed out his window toward the runway and Dave could see the grim look on his face. It was gone when he turned back.

"Alright, Lieutenant, have the report on my desk by noon and I'll see what I can do about getting you another plane. Dismissed." Dave saluted and left.

They found Dave and the crew another plane after they were given several days' leave and they flew sorties every day without seeing another single enemy submarine.

It was a month to the day he had arrived in Nova Scotia that he received orders to report to Halifax Harbor, Pier 21. *This was it,* he thought. He would soon be in the thick of the fight with the Germans. His letter to Julia that day was very sad.

Dear Julia,

Honey, I just received my orders to Pier 21, which means I'm about to head to England. Probably by the time you get this, I'll be there. I miss you so much, I sometimes even think of just heading back to you, but that would never do. I yearn for the day that I can hold you in my arms again and feel your soft body next to mine. I'm still not used to being called Lieutenant, but it is kind of nice. Well, I've got so much to say, but no time to put it into words. Pray for me and know that you will be with me wherever I am, all the time.

All my love, Dave.

Dave also said his farewells to the crew whom he had come to regard as great friends as well as airmen. As he stood in the tiny chapel, he said a prayer for them and a goodbye to Lieutenant Wayne.

xxxxxxxxxxxxxxxxxxxxxxxxxxxxxxxxxxxxxxxxxxxx

Dave was sick for the first few days at sea. Before this, he hadn't been on a body of water any bigger than Montreal Lake, but now, since they had left Halifax Harbour, he had not been able to sight land anywhere and they were still forming up the convoy. He, as well as many of the other airmen, continued to be sick after their ship started slowly chugging eastward and for the last twenty hours, most of the waves seemed to him to be the size of mountains. He had never seen so much water except from the air and was sure he would never want to see it again. Many of the men who were sick were worse off than he, simply because they didn't have anything in their stomachs to throw up and so they had dry heaves. Dave tried to eat small amounts, even though he soon had to chuck it. The problem was further acerbated by the fact that they were in convoy. Many of the ships had to go slowly because of the high seas, and the convoy could move only as fast as the slowest ship.

Finally, after the third day, the ocean was somewhat calmer and Dave, along with most of the others, began to feel better. He even ventured above deck for some fresh air with a group of flyers. The wind had calmed, although there was still a stiff breeze from the movement of the ship. The convoy had now picked up speed. He counted twenty-two merchant marine ships that he could see and spotted what he thought were two Royal Canadian Navy destroyers. He also picked out two of the navy's smaller corvettes. Dave watched while a corvette cruised by, going in the opposite direction from the ship he was on. He had been told that they were real workhorses for the Canadian Navy.

As he watched the ships zigzagging, he mused about the fact that the American president, Franklin T. Roosevelt, had been unsuccessful so far in leading his country into the war, due to strong pacifist lobbies and in some higher-up quarters - even Nazi sympathizers - but he had found a way to support the Brits through Lend Lease. His garden hose story had helped keep Britain afloat with supplies and most of these ships were carrying the material across the ocean.

Just as he stepped towards the door leading off the deck to return to his berth, he noticed out of the corner of his eye that one of the merchantmen off to the north suddenly erupted in flames. There were the terrible few seconds of horrified disbelief and then the sound of the explosion. Dave watched as the two destroyers and two corvettes suddenly made hard turns and went to battle stations. The four escort ships increased speed and began laying down a blanket of smoke around the convoy. The group that Dave was in, who had been enjoying the fresh air, was ordered below deck and later they heard and felt the vibrations of depth charges as the Canadian war ships chased the U-boats. If the U-boat managed to escape the RCN escorts, they must have chosen to find other prey because that was their last attack on this convoy.

It was November 22, 1941 when a group of the airmen let out a hoorah from the deck of the troop ship. They had spotted the coastline of what they would soon find out was Scotland. The next day, Dave and six hundred other airmen and soldiers disembarked in Glasgow, Scotland. They had no sooner touched Scottish soil than the airmen were loaded onto a passenger train and for the next four hours, they slowly moved toward the 419 squadron's base at Middleton St. George, Teeside. If any of the men thought that they had finished training back in Canada, they quickly found out that this was where training really began. Probably the most difficult lesson was the currency. They had heard the terms: shilling, pence, quid, halfpenny, pound, farthing, florin, crown and guinea, but the problem was to make any sense out of it all. Dave was told that the easiest way was to just use the British money and not try to compare it to Canada's currency. As it turned out, he was getting paid much more than his British counterpart, but much less than his equal in the American Air Force.

The Purple Heart Bride
Chapter 6

Dave entered the barracks at Middleton to find that they were damp and cool, heated only by a small coal heater which was grossly undersized for the area. The bunks were spartan with a two-inch mattress and the bedding consisted of sheets, pillow and a woollen blanket. If anyone thought that the showers would be a reprieve, they were sorely disappointed because the water was ice cold. Dave imagined ice forming on the cement floor while he showered.

He found that his time flying in the jump seat of a Halifax was better and more comfortable, not that he had a choice. On his off hours, he wrote letters to Julia and also began to spend more time at the officers' club. He enjoyed meeting the different airmen and listening to their stories. He also found that the alcohol helped quiet his nerves, but did nothing to make him feel warm so he could sleep through the cold nights. The only thing that helped him feel warm and truly settle his nerves was thinking of Julia. It was nearly two weeks before he received his first letter from her. She had written it long before he left Shearwater, but the mail had been delayed.

Dear Dave,

Honey I love you and miss you. I got your letter that you might be transferred and felt a huge part of me go numb. I hope you're sitting down while reading this because I've got some great news. The doctor informed me that there is to be a new addition to our family. I want to call him David Jr., but will wait to see what you say. If it's a girl, I'd like Barbara. It's going to be a boy though - I know it. Maybe you could get leave and travel home when the baby is born. That is, if you're still in Canada. The weather has turned more chilly - especially for late September. No matter. I'm warm with the feeling that you will return to me safely. I know now that you will because you have to see your son. Did I tell you I love you? Well there, I said it again. I love you and miss you and can't wait until you come home.

All my love, Julia xoxoxoxoxoxoxo.

Dave folded the letter and as he reminisced about his girl, his eyes filled with tears and he yearned to be with her. He sat in a somber mood, thinking about her until a large aircraft flew over the barracks and shook him from his reverie.

Shaken back to the present, he hurried around and told all his new friends the good news. When at last he settled down, he wrote Julia back. He told her that the name David would be OK and he always liked the name Barbara, so that was fine if it was a girl.

xxxxxxxxxxxxxxxxxxxxxxxxxxxxxxxxxxxxxxxxxxxxxxx

Within the week, he was ordered to put together a crew. Dave hurried to the club, where he hoped he would be able to talk seven guys into flying with him. When he entered the room, the first person he saw was a man up on a table doing a tap dance. *"Now how the hell did he get here?"* He made his way to the front of the crowd.

"George, when the hell did you arrive?" he said. George almost fell off the table, partly because he was drunk and partly from the surprise of seeing his best friend, but he held his wide smile and managed to jump down.

"Wow, Dave, I didn't know you were here. I got in day before yesterday. They had me in the brig for taking a swing at an officer," he said with an impish grin. When Dave frowned he continued. "Well, how the hell was I to know the guy was an officer? He was in civvies." Dave steered him over to a table and sat him down, retrieved a couple of Canadian Clubs with Coke and began to give him the spiel of flying with him in his crew. He was halfway through when George managed to stand up.

"Master Sergeant George Waters reporting for duty Sir." George saluted Dave as he half fell, half sat down again. "I'm your navigator, Dave." Then George pointed to a group of men. "I met those fellas coming over from Canada and they're all swell guys." He waved at a tall lanky man to come over and the man stepped up to the table.

"Flight Engineer Officer, Jack Clemens, meet my best friend and a man looking for a good engineer." George said. Dave stared at the man with a worried look. Dave talked to him awhile and told him he had flown combat a bit, but he had his orders to put together a crew.

"Uh, well, I mean, do you think you'll be able to fly under fire Sir?" Jack asked.

"I understand your concern Jack. That big plane has lots of complicated switches, levers, dials and stuff, but I figure if you tell me what they're all for, maybe we can get'er off the ground." That broke the ice and Jack could hardly stop laughing long enough to agree to sign on. By now, the others were standing around the table and Dave was going to give his speech to each of them when someone yelled from the corner of the room by the big stand up radio.

"Hey Roosevelt is about to make a speech. They said it's something about the Japanese bombing Hawaii." The pilot turned up the radio and all else in the room went quiet.

"Mr. Vice President, Mr. Speaker, Members of the Senate, and of the House of Representatives:

Yesterday, December 7th, 1941 -- a date which will live in infamy -- the United States of America was suddenly and deliberately attacked by naval and air forces of the Empire of Japan.

The United States was at peace with that nation and, at the solicitation of Japan, was still in conversation with its government and its emperor looking toward the maintenance of peace in the Pacific.

Indeed, one hour after Japanese air squadrons had commenced bombing in the American island of Oahu, the Japanese ambassador to the United States and his colleague delivered to our Secretary of State a formal reply to a recent American message. And while this reply stated that it seemed useless to continue the existing diplomatic negotiations, it contained no threat or hint of war or of armed attack.

It will be recorded that the distance of Hawaii from Japan makes it obvious that the attack was deliberately planned many days or even weeks ago. During the intervening time, the Japanese government has deliberately sought to deceive the United States by false statements and expressions of hope for continued peace.

The attack yesterday on the Hawaiian Islands has caused severe damage to American naval and military forces. I regret to tell you that very many American lives have been lost. In addition, American ships have been reported torpedoed on the high seas between San Francisco and Honolulu."

Jack began to turn a paler white, grabbed George's drink and downed it.

"Hey Jack, what the hell's the matter with you?" George yelled.

"The Japs bombed Oahu. My brother is

assigned to the Arizona there. The last thing he said to me was I was crazy to join up in Canada instead of joining our own air force. Now he's been caught in a surprise attack," Jack said in a low scream.

"Hey keep it down would you; I want to hear this," someone from the other corner of the room yelled and again the speech took center stage.

"*Hostilities exist. There is no blinking at the fact that our people, our territory, and our interests are in grave danger.*

With confidence in our armed forces, with the unbending determination of our people, we will gain the inevitable triumph -- so help us God.

I ask that the Congress declare, that since the unprovoked and dastardly attack by Japan on Sunday, December 7th, 1941, a state of war has existed between the United States and the Japanese empire."

The announcer came on and reiterated, "You have just heard the President of the United States and his speech to the American House of Representatives and Senate. The United States is now at war with Japan."

"What do you figure that means, Dave? George asked.

"I don't really know, but it might end Lend Lease. They're probably going to want that stuff for the Pacific now." Dave was still sitting and had hardly raised his head when he was almost face-to-face with one of the men.

"Corporal William Metcaff, Sir, I'd be proud to be your tail gunner and I'll watch your behind," he said in a very serious tone. Immediately, George and then everyone else broke out laughing and Billy gave George a push to shut him up. "I mean, I'll keep the German fighters off our back, Sir," he said, as he sneered at the group, sticking his tongue out at them. He saluted Dave, who returned the salute.

"Little short aren't you? You sure you're old enough to be out all night?" Dave jested.

"Nineteen, Sir and short is a plus for tail gunner." Dave nodded his agreement and approval. Dave could see that the next man liked his food. He made eye contact with the red-haired man to indicate that he was next.

"Corporal Terrance Barnes here Sir - I'll be your wireless operator. Never lost a radio yet Sir," he said with a jolly chuckle. Dave returned his salute and nodded. As if an inner voice spoke load and clear, Dave got the immediate feeling that the person now moving toward him was of a different breed than the rest.

"Sergeant Robert Griffith, Sir. I'd be your mid gunner," Bob said, with total self-assurance and a look that screamed, *don't mess with me*. Dave nodded to him as the last man stepped forward. Dave could see he was the old man of the group.

"Master Sergeant Charles Jones, Sir - Bomb aimer and front gunner." Charley shook Dave's hand. "Good luck with the controls, Sir. I hope you get them all figured out *before* we try to leave the ground," he said with a wide grin. Dave scanned the group with a smile.

"I couldn't have picked a better group if I tried," he said, as he rolled his eyes. "So have any of you seen an empty Halifax kicking around? I think the name on the front was Jenny. The number was…" (he pulled his orders from his jacket pocket) "RV769. That's the one we're supposed to fly." Terry moved forward, saluted again and was just about to answer Dave's question, when Dave cut him off.

"Look guys, when we're not in the company of other military, especially higher ranks, I'd appreciate it if we just used first names and put a hold on the sirs and salutes. I figure we're a team; we all have a job to do and we pretty much know what that is. My job is different from Jack's and Jack's job is different from Terry's. I'm in command, but I also take orders, so let's keep those kinds of things as our way of doing things. Besides, you don't need to salute in here anyway." Everyone looked at each other and George was smiling at the others as if to say, I told you so. Dave turned to Terry and nodded for him to continue.

"I think that's the one over in Hanger Number Three. I heard it came in a few weeks ago all shot up and the only survivor was the flight engineer. He brought it in. They've been working on it ever since."

"Well then, we better go see this aircraft and starting right now, its history will change," he said, as he motioned for the rest to follow him and marched out the door in the direction of Hanger Number Three. The crew followed Dave across the tarmac to a huge hanger where, among other large bombers, a Halifax stood, with several unpainted patches newly applied to the fuselage. Dave noticed that the left engine had also been replaced, but had not yet been painted. Although maintenance men were swarmed all over the plane like ants on a disturbed anthill, Dave and his new crew were able to scramble into the fuselage and check out the huge plane. Each man took his position in the craft and double-checked the equipment. The hours quickly slipped away and by the time someone noticed the time, it was twenty-three hundred. Dave called the men together and suggested that they all get back to their barracks and get some sleep.

The next morning, Dave submitted his list and he and his new crew were awarded a smaller barracks that was amply heated and also had warm water. Shortly afterwards, he received his first assignment and filed the flight plans. They were to fly mock low-level bombing runs along the coast and test as well as get the feel of the equipment. When Dave asked how long the crew would be practising like this, the duty officer grunted, "As long as it's bloody necessary.

Dave and the crew took their stations in the craft and Dave taxied to the end of the appointed runway. As they sat at the approach, Dave and Jack ran through a preliminary take-off check. They had barely completed their check, when the tower gave him clearance and Dave pulled out onto the runway and stopped. He lowered the flaps to five percent, spooled the engines to thirty percent and then released the brake. The huge plane began to roll while Dave fought to keep it straight and once he had gained perfect control, he pushed the four throttles to take-off speed while continuing to keep the aircraft straight with the rudder. The Halifax lumbered down the runway with vibrations and wheel noise. It slowly picked up speed and Dave wasn't sure it would ever produce enough speed to get airborne, but a little over half-way down the strip, the huge bird's tires slowly lifted off of the ground and suddenly all the vibrations stopped. He raised the landing gear and leveled the flaps while gradually gaining altitude. Dave pulled back a little on the yoke and the Halifax responded with a slight increase in upward elevation. By now they were at fifteen hundred feet and there was a cheer from the crew in the back.

"I'd give all the credit to Jack here. He's been continually nattering about what to do and what not to touch. He says landing is even more difficult," Dave said as he chuckled into his microphone.

"Did I mention to you guys that our fearless pilot crashed and destroyed a very nice Harvard back in Canada?" George added.

"Hey Captain, if you're going to crash this thing, put the nose in first. Don't drag the tail whatever you do." Billy said and snickered from his lonely compartment at the back end of the plane, but everyone could tell he was nervous.

"Relax guys. When I land this jalopy back in merry old England, you won't even feel the bump."

Things quieted down for a long while until they were over the ocean at ten thousand feet.

"Captain, can I test these Brownings?" Bob requested.

"Yeah, I'd like to try mine too," Billy chimed in. Dave had no sooner given them the go-ahead than he could hear Bob's 303 machine guns and Charles' pair of nose guns rattling with their staccatos and then after a little under thirty seconds, they quickly went silent again.

"These babies are working fine," Billy said, with excitement in his voice.

For the next half-hour, Charles, Jack and Dave kept a running conversation about where they had grown up. Charles was from a ranch south of Calgary. That would ordinarily have earned him the nickname of cowboy, except for the fact that he was the guy who aimed the bombs. Someone suggested you don't mess with the marshal and the name stuck. Jack was a yank from Waco

Texas. He had decided he couldn't wait for his native country to get into the war so had crossed the border and signed up. Now that Japan had attacked Pearl Harbor, he had to do a lot of soul-searching, but something kept telling him that he could fight the Axis with a Canuck crew just as easily as he could with an American, so he had decided to stay on.

"Okay skipper, we're coming up to north fifty-seven degrees latitude. You need to drop down to five thousand feet and make the run over the town," George said calmly into his face-piece.

"Roger, navigator. Hang on fellas," Dave said, as he slowly cut power and moved the yoke ahead. The Halifax responded, with the nose dipping dramatically. The aircraft picked up considerable speed and then, as it got close to the required altitude, Dave pulled back on the yoke and leveled off. "We're at altitude, navigator."

"Okay skipper, turn to heading 360 degrees and we will fly right over our target."

"Roger, navigator, coming to 360 degrees," Dave said, moving to full flaps and slowly pushing the throttle ahead as the plane slowed, but held its altitude. Jack stared at the gauges.

"Where did you learn to do that? We're barely moving and not losing any altitude," Jack said, amazed. "We're not going to stall are we?"

"A fellow in a Lancaster back in Canada showed me how to do it," Dave said with a grin.

"Figured it would give Charles an easy time to spot the target." He held his mask to his face.

"Okay, Bomb Aimer, I'm turning the plane over to you."

"Roger, Captain, I've got control," Charles said.

Five minutes later, the controls were switched back to Dave. He zeroed the flaps incrementally and cut the throttles back to cruise while gently gaining altitude. He then made a large 180-degree turn to head back to Middleton. After flying out over the channel for nearly an hour, Dave banked hard and, following the bearing that George had given him, flew west toward the home airstrip. After receiving a green light to land, Dave set full flaps and slowly let the Halifax settle towards the ground. There was a slight jerk when the wheels touched the pavement and then the aircraft rumbled down the strip with the tail wheel finally touching down. Dave applied enough brake to slow to taxi speed and then brought the plane around to its place by hanger number three. The ground crew, friendly as always, gathered around as Dave's men exited the aircraft.

"Ow's the ol' girlie flyin' Lieutenant?" Sergeant Rudy Dickerson of the British ground crew inquired after saluting. "Did she give ye any problems sir?"

"Flew like a dove, Sergeant. She'll hold altitude at eighty-five miles per hour, full flaps, carriage down," Dave said. The sergeant took a step back in amazement and then took a minute to do some computing on a piece of scrap paper from his shirt pocket. He began to smile as he finished.

"Beggin' yer pardon Sir, but y' must be mistakin'. The Halifax is rated for a stall speed of 144 kilometres per hour and my figurin' says that's ninety miles per hour. So ya see, Sir, it's impossible. At eighty-five you would av' come down like a brick." Jack walked up to the pair and nodded toward Dave.

"It was eighty-five, Sergeant and the skipper here never lost a foot of altitude for ten minutes. He even gave the bomb aimer the plane for five minutes and then when we finished the run, he lifted away like a gull that grabs the waft of a breeze." The sergeant had an incredulous expression on his face. He had just found a new national hero to worship.

"Well I s'pose if the lieutenant 'ere and 'is engineer both say it's so, it must be. It'll be somethin' to tell the missus it will," he said, more or less talking to himself as he headed for his toolbox.

The next day, the crew went on another practice mission, but this time they were to fly at a very low altitude and simulate dropping mines into the water. Dave again used the maneuver to slow the plane down just before the drop, but this time, due to the very low altitude, he kept the airspeed just above the specified stall speed.

xxx

Completing all the maneuvers required, Dave flew back to base and brought the plane to its appointed hanger.

Dave noticed a couple of officers on the tarmac near the hanger that he was headed for and when he brought the Halifax in front of the large doors, he saw that a Lancaster was inside. He shut down the Halifax and as he joined the crew on the ground, one of the officers stepped over to him.

"Lieutenant Lysik?"

"Yes, Sir," Dave said with a salute. The officer returned his salute.

"We have decided we would like you and your crew to begin training on this Lanc. here. You will begin familiarization starting tomorrow 0400. Your flight plan is ready for you."

"Yes Sir. May I ask why, Sir?"

"It probably has something to do with some training you had on the bird's sister ship back in Canada. You've got more time on it than anyone here. 0400, Lieutenant." The officer saluted and without waiting for Dave's return salute, swung around and returned to the other two officers, who then headed in the direction of the base command.

George shuffled over to Dave.

"What's with the brass? They don't generally come out to welcome us home. And what's that new Lanc doing in the hanger?"

"That new Lanc is our new bomber and the officer was just personally giving us our orders for tomorrow, early. We start training on it at 0400." George looked at the newly painted aircraft and then ran over to the rest of the crew who were in a group admiring the new plane. He excitedly repeated what Dave had told him. They returned to the barracks with even more camaraderie than usual.

They got cleaned up and then headed for the beer hall. It was December 11, 1941, and the whole crew was concerned about their first Christmas in this distant land, so they thought that some fun would help clear the homesickness. As they stepped inside the door, it was obvious that something had happened. Everyone had a smile a mile wide and there was an air of celebration that was impossible to miss.

"What's going on?" Dave asked the British barkeep. The man chuckled.

"Oh, it's marvelous, it is, my good man. That little Bohemian corporal across the channel there 'as declared war with America. Sounds like the Japanese signed a pact with Hitler before they bombed Hawaii. That means, seeing's 'ow America is at war with Japan, they are also at war with Germany. That means we might get all the help we need to get rid of the little tramp," he said with his smile almost lighting up the beer hall. "You know, somehow I think ol' Roosevelt had this all worked out. Hitler said having Japan on his side is a good omen. He says the Japanese haven't lost a war in 1500 years. Anyway, it gets the Yanks into the fray and that's very good news for us." Dave caught the eye of each one of his crew and motioned for them to find a table. He singled Jack out and led him to the side.

"If you want to repatriate with your fellow countrymen, I and the crew will hold no bad feelings," Dave said, as sincerely as he could. Jack stared back at him with a grin.

"Dave, if you're going to get that big bird in the air, I figure you will need me to tell you where all those complicated switches and levers are. We can't win this thing if the pilots are left alone to crash the damn planes," Jack said with his best Cockney accent. Dave laughed and slapped him on the back.

"Hey guys, the Texas Ranger here says he's with us for the duration." A cheer went up as all seven airmen toasted with a fresh mug of ale.

Christmas was a lonely time for most of the men. For the greatest majority of them, this was their first time away from home and especially at Christmas. Therefore, when a Christmas party and candlelight service was scheduled for December 24, everyone who was not doing century duty or KP attended. As Dave's crew entered the huge hanger they saw that the whole place was decorated with Christmas ornaments and in the middle was a large four-engine Lancaster.

"Wow!" Billy exclaimed, as he scanned the huge area with hundred airforce personnel milling around. The crew immediately realized that almost everyone was carrying a paper cup with presumably more than soda pop in it.

Dave, Jack and Billy moved over to the Lancaster and spent a lot of time just looking the plane over. George, Charles, Terry and Bob, on the other hand, proceeded to fill their cups with liquor and drink it as fast as they could. As they sat around a circular table, they, for the most part, were in a jovial mood.

"Hey Shorje, I doen't think they put an, any al co hol in this snuff," Terry said with a slur. Bob looked at the young man with disdain.

"Damn, I don't know why they let kids in here to screw up the evening," Bob sneered. Terry clamored to his feet and unsteadily pointed at Bob.

"Whooch you callin a, a kid?" Terry asked and then collapsed to the floor overcome by the alcohol. Charles and George helped Terry back to the barracks and decided to find a different area of the hanger than where Bob was, to spend the rest of the evening.

Much later, a Christian Service was held where everyone on base - except Terry, that is - was able to worship and celebrate the birth of his Savior. Most of the men were stone sober when they returned to their barracks and many, like Dave, chose that time to write a letter to their loved ones.

The weeks flew by and the crew became a unit, being able to anticipate each others next move and work together as one. That is, all except Bob, the mid-ship gunner. He was a loner and had no thought of joining in with the others.

It was after a practice flight, near the end of May that the trouble started. The crew found a small-town pub to quench their thirst. Bob had sauntered up to a very attractive young woman, while the rest of the crew sat at a table and watched to see what would happen. He started talking to her in a vulgar manner, as was his way. He didn't know, nor did he care, that the young lady had an escort. When her young man returned, Bob challenged him and words ensued - very course and loud words - all coming from Bob. Dave decided he had better defuse the situation quickly before Bob started swinging.

As Dave sidled up to the angry men, Bob took a swing at the boyfriend. The boyfriend ducked and the fist caught Dave by surprise, sending him several steps back before he crashed over a table. As the crew leader hit the floor, unconscious, two of the locals grabbed Bob while some other patron toughs used him for punching practice. Of course, the crew couldn't allow that and jumped into the fight. Before anyone could bring the melee under control, the entire population of the pub was breaking chairs, tables and people. The local police arrived at the same time as the MPs and within short order, the crew of the Jenny were shackled and escorted back to the base's brig. They were all locked into a single cell until the wing commander was summoned.

"Well sergeant, I hope you're happy. I'm just going to love trying to tell my parents why I have to spend two years behind bars instead of fighting the bloody Germans," Billy said defiantly.

"Ah close your trap, you little fart," Bob responded with a sneer. Billy jumped to his feet and was rushing over towards Bob, when Dave stepped in front of him. He stopped Billy by putting his hands on the young man's chest and motioned for the lad to take his seat. When he was sure that the tail gunner had complied, he stepped towards Bob, who, with a smirk on his face, was still seated.

"Sergeant Griffiths! You will come to attention," Dave barked and when Bob didn't respond he growled, "Now, Sergeant." Bob came to his feet in a relaxed way and stepped forward, more as a challenge than at attention. Dave made eye contact and Bob stared blankly into his superior's eyes with a wicked, rebellious look. Dave took one more step towards the man, bringing him within six inches from the sergeant. Dave noticed that Bob was setting up to bring a fist up into Dave's midsection, but Dave's fist, doing the same thing, got to its target first and drove the air out of the sergeant's lungs. With Bob's air evacuated, his punch came to nothing and as he bent forward, Dave lifted a knee into the sergeant's face. Dave quickly grabbed the sagging man and held him up.

"Terry, would you help me sit the good sergeant down?" Dave said with a seemingly sympathetic growl. "I think he must have been injured more severely in the fight he started this evening than we had supposed." No one actually saw what Dave had done, not even Bob. Of course, Bob and everyone else knew exactly what had happened.

Dave called the guard and explained that he believed Sergeant Griffith might be in need of medical attention. Bob, with a cloth mostly soaked with his blood and holding it to his face, was escorted to the infirmary by two burly mps, where he was stitched up and checked out.

When Wing Commander More stepped into the guardhouse and up to the cell, he motioned to the guard at his side.

"Bring Lieutenant Lysik along. I'll have words with him," he said and he turned and left for an office outside of the cell area. Dave entered the office shortly after the wing commander, and was told to stand at attention in front of the desk. The wing commander moved behind the desk and sat down. He let a few moments go before he raised his eyes to glare at Dave.

"Okay, Lysik, what in hell do you and your crew

think you're doing? A brawl in an English pub - can't you keep your boys under control better than that?" Dave gazed at the wing commander, who was shockingly well-built and really didn't seem old enough to have reached that height of command. "Well, what's the matter, cat got your tongue?" the officer snapped.

"There is no excuse for such behaviour and I've told my men that in no uncertain terms, Sir."

"Yeah, I saw the one you spoke to. I think he'll be okay, but I don't think he'll be any good in your crew after this. He was the instigator wasn't he?" the wing commander asked.

"Yes Sir, he's been the sore thumb of the outfit from the first. Tonight was just a sample of where he's headed."

Commander More glanced at Dave and then stood to walk around the room with his hands behind his back.

"I'll see to it that Sergeant Griffith is reassigned and you and your men will be released," he said. "But I need your assurance that this kind of thing will not happen again."

"Yes Sir. You have that assurance Sir. Our crew wants to fight the Germans - not the English," Dave said with a smile.

"Lysik, be in my office at 0530 tomorrow and for God's sake, do something about that eye."

"Yes Sir," Dave replied as he gave a sharp salute and turned in his best form to exit the room.

The Purple Heart Bride
Chapter 7

Lieutenant Lysik had just stepped outside the door of the barracks onto the gravel walk, heading for the wing commander's office, when a man with Royal Australian Air Force patches walked briskly up to him. The tall, slim man wore the stripes of a sergeant and made a half-step right in front of Dave, then sprung to attention with a snappy, perfect salute.

"Morning Sir," he said with almost a Cockney accent, but different. "I'd be lookin' fir the Flight Lieutenant Lysik, Sir."

"You've found me, Sergeant. What can I do for you?"

"Sergeant Ronald Brown, Royal Australian Air Force, reporting fir duty Sir. I was told to report as mid-gunner, Sir." Dave quickly tried to assess this man.

"*Well, the replacement certainly looks better than the original,*" he thought.

"Sergeant, go on in and meet the crew. I've got other pressing matters to attend to right now, but afterwards, I'd like a few words." He turned and left without another word. Sergeant Brown stood for a moment, wondering about his new lieutenant and then, due to the fact that he was now standing alone, said to himself, "Thank-you... Sir."

As the minute hand of the big clock on the wall

moved to 0530, Dave stepped up to the corporal's desk.

"I was ordered to see Wing Commander More," Dave said.

"Third door on your right," the corporal said as he pointed down the hallway. "They're waiting for you." Dave raised his eyebrows at this revelation. *They?*

He entered the large office and was shaken by the number of high ranking officers seated around the room. The only one he recognized was Wing Commander Moore but he didn't miss the insignias. There was a British air commodore, two American generals, a man in what looked to be an expensive suit and a lady in stylish clothes.

Great, I suppose these are the two from the pub the other night. Must be royalty by the amount of brass in here. He figured that now was the time to give his most sincere salute.

"Flight Lieutenant Lysik reporting as ordered Sir," he barked as his arm bent at exactly the right angle and his fingers stopped at the brim of his hat.

"At your ease Flight Lieutenant." Before Dave could complete the move to his at-ease stance, a chair was placed in front of him to sit in. The chair was positioned in such a manner that he faced all but the wing commander. Commander Moore got up and moved to within Dave's vision.

"Alright then, I suppose first off, I should tell you the reason you're here. We have an extremely dangerous and sensitive mission, which will be on a volunteer basis. Are you willing to go above and beyond the call of duty, Flight Lieutenant?"

"Yes sir," Dave said without hesitation.

"Good, you will have to give your crew the same option when you get back to the barracks. Of course, you will not tell them what that mission will be."

"Yes Sir."

"Alright then. I'll introduce these officers and then get to the reason we're here." He motioned with an outstretched hand to one of the Americans. This is General Burgess USAF. Next to him is British Air Commodore Guthrie." He made eye contact with the young lady. "This lady with the flaming red hair will have the code-name of Commander Hood and the gentleman with her will have the code-name Mr. Wolf. Dave noticed that the code-name would surely fit him as he was big and he gave the aura of being bad.

"And last," he said as he grinned, "but by no means least, General Burrows USAF." The wing commander walked back behind his desk and sat down and Commodore Guthrie took over.

"The problem is this then," he said. "We need to gather some intelligence. Some very specific intelligence that we're sure Jerry keeps completely under wraps. We're going to need pictures from the air and information from the ground." He motioned for the wing commander to close the blinds and he flipped the lights off as he walked over to a map on the wall that was left illuminated. He tapped a wooden pointer on the map.

"Right here is Gottow, little town south of Berlin where we have unsubstantiated intelligence Jerry is very active doing something. We could blow the place to kingdom come, but first we would like to find out just what the little tramp is up to. On the other hand, if he gets an inkling that we know anything about it, he'd probably demolish it himself and move it someplace else. That's where you come in." He nodded toward Dave, "Your flight reports are very impressive. We want you to fly a bombing mission, but that will only be a diversion. After you drop your bombs on a critical target in a real bombing raid, you divert to another zone and will drop our people in there," he nodded toward the lady and gentleman, "we want them to jump very high and very slow. We want them in close proximity to each other when they hit the ground. Then with that completed, you move to your final part of the mission. You will acquire some low level reconnaissance pictures of what we believe is a very nasty place. I'm sure you'll get more than your share of ground fire, but the whole mission is double "A" strategic." He nodded his head and raised his eyebrows. "Do you think you and your crew are up to this mission, Lieutenant?" Dave stared at the map, then at the people, then back at the map and finally at the commodore.

"Why, yes Sir! If anyone can do it, my crew can."

"Good man. Now for reasons that are obvious, this mission is strictly volunteer for you and your men so you must give them the same option of volunteering. Further, fortunately, your boys have had their night out, because you will all have to be sequestered until the mission is completed. Also, we have determined that between now and the final briefing, Commander Hood will fly at least one training mission, maybe more, at her discretion, to ensure complete readiness. Your mission is tentatively scheduled for 1830 hours, 14 June. That gives you and your men awhile to prepare."

Now the tall, lean American General Burrows stood.

"The key here is secrecy. One hint of this gets out to the Germans and the whole mission will be a disaster as well as useless. The people that drop in will be at great risk at any rate, but if our plans are found out, it will mean certain death without the chance of any intel. Do I make myself clear, Lieutenant?" he said in a gruff no-nonsense voice. His stare was like flint and Dave could imagine it piercing right through him.

"Yes Sir!" was all Dave could manage to say.

Now the wing commander took over again.

"Alright then, Lieutenant, you will report to your barracks. You and your men will do some training with your new commander after which we will brief you and your crew." As Dave gazed around the room, the wing commander stood a little straighter.

"Dismissed, Lieutenant."

"Yes Sir," Dave said as he stood to attention and snapped his best salute, turned and left the office.

An MP escorted Dave back to the barracks, where two other burly MPs were stationed at the barracks door. As he approached, the slightly shorter guard stepped in front of Dave's path, suggestively blocking his entrance.

"Halt!" the shorter one barked. "I'll need to see ID sir." Dave passed his wallet to him and the shorter guard checked the credentials.

"Lieutenant Lysik?"

Dave just nodded.

"You the ranking officer of this crew?"

Dave nodded again.

"You may enter, but I have to inform you that no one will be allowed to leave this building without escort until further notice," the guard said in a more amiable voice. "Commander Moore's orders."

As the other M.P. shouldered his weapon, they both saluted. Dave returned the salute, stepped by the guards and entered the barracks. Once inside, he was immediately inundated by questions from the entire crew.

"What's going on, Captain?" asked Billy. Dave didn't answer, but ordered everyone to gather around the writing table. When the crew had settled down, Dave opened up a map.

"We have a mission over Germany. The brass will brief all of us later on specifics, but for now it's enough to know that this is extremely dangerous and extremely secret." Dave glanced at each of his men. "That means the mission is volunteer only. If anyone wants out, say so and no one will hold it against you."

Dave received a nod from each crew member without as much as a hesitation. He was really growing to admire these guys.

"Okay, so we'll get one practice flight with a colonel by the name of Hood and I might as well tell you now, because I'm sure you won't miss it, that this officer is a female. I'm also pretty sure she is Strategic Air Services, but outranks me, so she will be in command while she is with us."

Sergeant Brown rolled his eyes.

"A bloomin' Jane and I thought those SAS guys were supposed to be tough. Next thing you know, they'll have us practicing ballet on our tippy toes in Berlin." The guys all guffawed.

"Fellas, I think this little lady is just a little tougher than your normal Saturday night date. At any rate, I expect you to show her the respect her rank deserves and I think you'll realize she deserves that respect, once you see her in action." Dave hoped so anyway.

"That's all I'm going to tell you for now. You'll get a briefing on our practice and then before the mission so that's about it unless there are any questions." All the guys immediately raised their hands. Dave just smiled and waved his hand.

"Put your hands down. I'm not answering any more questions."

The crew all laughed and split up to return to what they were doing before Dave had arrived. Dave remained at the table and began to write Julia another letter.

Purple Heart Bride
Chapter 8

Dave lay on his cot with his fingers laced behind his head. His nerves were on edge. He had already run the mission through his mind a hundred times trying to ensure himself he wouldn't make any critical mistakes that might harm his men or the SAS people.

"*The SAS people - what the hell were they up to?*" he thought.

He was surprised when he glanced around the barracks and everyone but Billy Metcalf seemed to be fast asleep. His thoughts reverted to Julia. He wondered what she would be doing right now. He finally concluded that she very well might be changing diapers on his new son or daughter. He spent a long time thinking about what the baby would look like.

"All babies pretty much look the same," he reckoned and then corrected himself. "Silly thought. Of course our baby will be the cutest little guy around and if it's a girl, she'll melt everyone's heart," he thought. With that, his mind returned to his sojourn in that brick building on the hill and how they had met. The corner of his lips turned up into a smile again as his mind replayed his first sight of her. Suddenly his heart felt like it might burst, so strong was the yearning to see her. He tried to work around this feeling of loss, but after a few minutes he knew it was useless. He got up, gathered some paper and a pencil and even though he knew he couldn't send it, began writing a letter to her.

Dear Jewel,

I figure you must have given birth to our new family member. I haven't received any mail for such a long time. I suspect it has something to do with what we're doing over here. We're flying a mission tomorrow and the thought of you and the new baby continue to fill my mind. My memories continually return to our first meeting. If you recall, I thought you were an angel and I had died and gone to heaven. I want you to know I still think of you as an angel, but I now realize the heaven you bring can be wherever I am; all I have to do is think about you.

My crew are all exceptional guys. George is my Navigator. Can you believe that? Mama always said he would lead me into trouble. Never fear sweet-heart, he's really good at telling us where we are and how to get to where we need to be. All but one of the guys are sleeping now as I should be, but I just had to write my feelings down for you.

I love you honey and I feel like if I don't see you soon I'm going to collapse. I guess there just isn't any words good enough to tell you how much I love you and how I miss you every day.

The weather here has been terrible but definitely better than at Christmas time. I don't know why they say merry old England. Seems

*the temperature never gets over sixty degrees
with a drizzle or fog most of the time. We do
however get sun a couple days of the week. It
doesn't stay. Give me Saskatchewan weather
any day. Well honey, I guess I'm just rambling so
I'll close for now and if they don't think I'm
sending any deep dark secrets you will know how
much I love and miss you. Until we're together
again.*

   All my love
   Dave

He folded the letter and after addressing the
envelope, closed it and carefully placed it in the
mail box by the door. He was well aware it
wouldn't go anywhere until his mission was
completed. He had no sooner finished than Billy
shuffled over to him. Dave could see the
consternation on the young man's face.

"Hey Corporal, you should be getting some
shuteye. We've got some heavy training ahead,"
Dave quietly said.

"Sir, I can't sleep. My mind keeps replaying that
crash this afternoon and it keeps telling me I'm
not going to make it through our first mission.
What should I do, Sir?"

"You got a girl, Billy?"

"Yeah, well sort of."

"Well, why don't you write her a letter and tell
her how much you care for her. I guarantee that if
your mind is on her, it won't be telling you lies
about not making it through the mission." Billy's

demeanor lightened a bit and he grabbed some paper and the pencil Dave had just left.

Dave went back to his cot and within minutes, was fast asleep. It seemed as though he had just laid down when someone jostled him.

"Lieutenant Lysik, time to get up Sir," Billy said. As Dave focused on the young tail gunner he saw that the man looked refreshed.

"So did the letter relax you and let you get some sleep?" Dave asked.

"Well, it did relax me, but I never slept a wink. On the other hand, my mind isn't telling me I won't make it through the mission either." Dave nodded to him and then with a loud voice, ordered the crew to get up and get dressed.

Each crew member put on three sets of socks and donned equally heavy pants and jackets. Finally, with parachutes in hand and an MP escort close by, they made their way to the hanger. As they headed into the hanger, the entire crew came to a halt and stood at the entrance to the cavernous building. It was a Lancaster and each man noticed that the new bomber seemed to have an aura around it.

Then they noticed the woman commander, known only as Commander Hood, as she was standing near the hatch. She was outfitted in dark field fatigues and carrying a parachute, but Dave could see that they didn't miss her figure. He thought he better act quickly, before one of the guys whistled or did something even more lewd.

She smiled as Lieutenant Lysik saluted.

"OK Lieutenant, I hope we're giving you enough time to become accustomed to this aircraft, but our planners decided we needed to use a Lancaster. They said they have a better range and more lift. I heard you've had previous training on it. Do you think you'll have a problem?" she asked. Dave glanced at the plane and then over to Jack.

"Naw, my engineer shows me what all the complicated stuff is for. I really like pulling and pushing the steering wheel." He winked at Jack. "You think you can get this one figured out, Jack?" he asked. Jack responded with his own humor.

"I figure we should be all right. I hear tell all you have to do is face these babies into the wind and they lift off and if not, as you can see they have really big fans on the wings." The commander chuckled and shook her head.

"Ah yes. I can see we're going to have a barrel of laughs on this one," she said lightly and then changed her voice to start spitting words like a machine gun. "Lieutenant!" she snapped. "Have your men attend their stations and check their equipment. You and your *engineer* can run through your pre-flight check." She stared at him, while seeming to see right through him. "I do not tolerate any tomfoolery. We leave that here right now. Do you understand that Mr. Lysik?"

Dave was taken by complete surprise by this

sudden turn of her demeanor.

"Yes Sir, Ah, I mean Ma'am." He stood dazed and gave a feeble salute as she turned and with a quick step, marched off toward an office in the hanger.

Dave and the crew went through pre-flight while waiting for their passenger. Dave glanced out his side window and saw Commander Hood come out of the hanger with Mr. Wolf and two other SAS members and wondered if she expected to bring them along as well. His answer was affirmative as all four boarded the aircraft. Dave started the four engines, each in its turn and ran them up. Once they had all smoothed out, he began moving toward the airstrip and received clearance just as he reached the approach.

The Lanc rumbled down the runway and soon was smooth and airborne. George gave Dave his headings and they set course for Scotland. The flight was cramped in the back and more or less boring on the flight deck. Commander Hood gave George the co-ordinates for the drop zone and told Dave to gain altitude to 20,000 feet.

Dave knew that this was a practice run and wondered if these people were actually going to jump from that far up. Dave knew that the ceiling for his aircraft was 24,500 and wasn't sure anyone could survive such a jump. He leveled off the large bomber just in time to hear George say they were five minutes to drop zone. With all his pilot skills, he slowed the aircraft down to just above air speed and then waited for the drop time. The bomb doors were opened and the bombardier called his bombs away.

Dave banked the Lanc in a large ninety-degree curve and headed across to the west side of the island. He traveled for a long while before losing enough altitude to remove the oxygen masks.

Commander Hood squeezed up to the flight deck.

"You certainly did a great job and there is only one change I want to make for the mission," she said.

"And what would that be, Commander?" Dave asked.

"After we jump, you will continue straight on, as if you never dropped us. I would say at least 20 minutes or so before you make the first ninety and then another 20 minutes before the second ninety. That should reduce the chance of the Nazis knowing what you were doing. Can you do that. Lieutenant?"

"Yes, ma'am," Dave said, "If that's what you want, then that is exactly what we will do," but he was thinking, "*Twenty minutes, 90 degrees, twenty minutes, 90 degrees and twenty minutes back. My god, she wants us to travel an extra hour before heading for the photo op. By the time we get there, it'll be mid-morning and we'll be sitting ducks.*"

The commander glanced at Dave with what

Dave thought to be a sympathetic look.

"Look Lieutenant, I know what you're thinking. This strategy will put you over Oswiecim later in the morning, but it is imperative we get in and get our information secretly if at all possible. I wouldn't ask you and your crew to do this if it wasn't absolutely necessary. So let's go through the practice again, using the straight out strategy." Dave repeated the order to the crew and then took the big bomber around for another pass. This was the second of four passes and as many hours. Finally, Commander Hood gave Dave the order to return to base.

The trip back to base was a quiet ride, with everyone doing their job as well as searching their inner thoughts about this secret, important mission coming up. Dave felt a pang of relief when he had the landing strip in sight and his mind was involved with landing the huge bomber. Dave brought the Lanc to a perfect landing and they were safely home, for now.

The Purple Heart Bride
Chapter 9

Dave watched his crew as they followed Commander Hood out and onto the tarmac. He could see that they were worn out and knew they would sleep soundly once they were in their bunks. Dave was the last to exit the Lanc and to say that he was testy was an understatement. All day, he had carried out orders to perform maneuvers that he considered asinine. He stared hard at the redhead. *Maybe I should just tell the little lady to go jump in the ocean and then take my time in the brig.*

"Lieutenant, I'll see you in my office in thirty minutes." Commander Hood said. Dave contained his desire to tell her what was on his mind.

"Certainly, Commander."

"Do you know where it is?"

"Certainly, Commander," he repeated in the same tone and gave a somewhat lazy salute.

Dave hardly noticed the cool water in the shower and was at the commander's office exactly on time. A corporal showed him in. As he stepped in the door, he was surprised to see Wing Commander Moore there and immediately thought the worst. *This is it*, he thought. *This is where my rank starts going backwards... Damn.*

"Come on in, Dave," Commander Hood said. Dave took a couple of steps and slapped a salute to the two officers and then stood at attention.

Hood moved behind her desk and then, smiling, nodded to Wing Commander Moore. He cleared his throat and stepped toward Dave.

"At ease, Lieutenant, the commander here has recommended you for another promotion," Moore said, as he handed him the double stripes of Captain. Son, I swear if we don't finish this damn war soon, at the rate you're going, you'll be giving me orders before it's over. He shook Dave's hand and congratulated him, as did Commander Hood.

"Thank you, Sir and Ma'am. I don't know what to say, except I'm not sure I deserve these."

"Take my word for it, Captain, you've earned them," Commander Hood said. You fly that aircraft as if it were an extension of your body. I know I gave you a pretty rough time up there today, but I had to know you were up to the job. This promotion is my way of saying you are. If anybody should have those stripes, you should." Dave felt a little sheepish as he considered the ill thoughts that he had harbored about the commander and with all the emotions running through his mind, his eyes became watery.

"Thank you again, Commander. Will that be all, Ma'am?"

"That's it, Captain, except get lots of rest and have you and your crew ready for briefing at 16:00 hours tomorrow. This is the real deal, Captain," she said, as if she'd done it a hundred times.

"Yes Ma'am." He snapped a salute, turned to the wing commander. "Sir." The two officers returned his salute and Dave wheeled, but then stopped and turned back to the two officers.

"You had a question, Captain?" Wing Commander Moore asked.

"Yes Sir, if possible I wonder if we could have the Lanc named the Blue Osprey? The two commanders glanced at each other and WC Moore allowed Commander Hood to respond.

"I'll see what we can do, Captain." With that, Dave again saluted and left the office.

   * * *

"You can't take that card. It's my turn," Billy yelled at George as George tried to slip a fast one past the young man.

"Oh, yeah, I guess you're right," George said with a grin.

"You know I'm darn right..." Billy trailed off as the barracks door swung open and a British corporal stepped in. He searched out Dave and saluted.

"Sir, the wing commander wants you and your crew at the briefing quonset in one hour." The corporal glanced at his watch. "That is to say, sixteen hundred hours, Sir."

"Thank you Corporal. We'll be there." His duty completed, the corporal saluted, turned and left. Dave scanned the room and as no one moved, he gave an order.

"You heard the man. This is it, guys. Get

yourselves ready and we'll learn all about our first real mission."

For the next forty minutes, the barracks was alive as the crew prepared. As they finished up, Dave moved towards the door and as he reached for the handle, he turned and gazed at his crew.

We're no longer the guys who, a year ago, were farm boys or city kids. We're a real honest-to-god, cohesive, fighting crew ready to do battle.

Dave led the group across the wide expanse of tarmac towards the briefing building. They were about half-way there when a Halifax appeared at the end of the runway to the south. They could hear the engines revving up, cough, sputter, slow down and misfire badly. The crew could see that the aircraft was trailing smoke. Dave also realized it was traveling much too fast. The landing gear didn't touch the pavement until the craft was far past the halfway marker of the runway. The men watched as the huge bomber suddenly skidded around to one side, collapsing the right-hand landing gear and allowing the wing to drop, rupturing the fuel tank. Almost instantly, the wing burst into flames.

As more and more of the bomber began to burn, Dave's crew could hear screams from the aircraft. The emergency fire crew hurried out onto the field and had just arrived at the crash site when the entire area was engulfed in a huge fireball. The red-orange flames towered a hundred feet in the air. It took a minute for Dave and his crew to comprehend what had just happened, but they could see that several of the firemen - who were still alive - were running aimlessly within the fire, while their clothing and hair were on fire. Dave felt sick to his stomach. He could now feel the heat of the fire as he watched the last fireman fall dead. Several of Dave's crew had already moved away from the group to throw up while the others stood helplessly watching and not quite believing their eyes. Finally, as a second fire crew rushed to the crash site, Dave turned to his crew.

"Fellas, I know this is terrible and may God be with those brave men, but we have to move on. The WC is waiting for us." Dave hoped that the grizly nature of the crash and foiled rescue would not inhibit his crew's ability to perform their own duties, although he knew that it would leave a mark on each of them that would never be erased.

In the lecture hall, Dave and his crew were directed to the front to fill the second row. The room was set up with four chairs on each side and an aisle running down the center. From front to back, there were ten rows. There was a slightly raised platform at the front with a lectern and a large illuminated map behind it. Dave noticed Mr. Wolf as well as a couple of others who appeared to be just as tough as he, sitting in the first row on the opposite side of the hall.

The WC came in a door by the platform with

General Burrows and Commander Hood. Moore picked up a pointer.

"Alright then, let's have quiet," the wing commander said while tapping on the lectern. He waited for absolute silence.

"Alright then, General Burrows and I will give you the overview of the plan and then ah, Commander Hood will give you specifics of her part of the operation. Gentlemen, from here on out and while you are in the air, until she has left you, she will be in charge of this operation. General, would you like to take it from here?" The WC proceeded to a chair at the corner of the platform and General Burrow moved to the map.

"OK, this is where these SAS people need to be delivered." He circled his pointer around an area just south of Berlin. "In this area near a town called Gottow. Also, we have reports - although not substantiated - that Hitler and his thugs are killing vast numbers of people of certain racial origins in a concentration camp over here." He pointed near Warsaw. "Now the problem is, if the Nazis get wind that we know anything about either - if in fact either is true - we believe they will destroy the installation our people want to investigate and ..."(he moved his pointer to the Warsaw area again) "possibly exterminate everyone in this... I might call it a concentration camp, which by the way has been rumored to be called Auschwitz after the small town next to it. So the overview of your mission will be, together with a good complement of other crews, to bomb a strategic target and then split off and proceed to the drop zone near Gottow where you will drop Commander Hood, Mr. Wolf and their friends." He directed attention to the three sitting in the front row. "Then you will double back for some early morning photography of the Auschwitz Camp. After completing a photographic run, you will make your way back to base." The general stopped for a moment to let what he had said sink in.

"Are there any questions?" Instantly, Ronald Brown's hand shot up and the general nodded to him.

"Well mate, aye wus just figurin'. All thet flyin around over there. Well, will the petrol hold out or do we wind up packing it in beyond the black stump." The general studied the young Aussie for a minute, thinking he was not showing proper respect to an officer, but caught himself and turned to Commander Moore.

"I'm not exactly sure what the question was. I think you want to know if the Lancaster can carry enough fuel to make it back home?" Sergeant Brown nodded. General Burrows nodded to Commander Moore.

"What about it, does the Lanc. carry enough fuel?" Moore stood and took a couple of steps to the front of the platform.

"Affirmative. That's why we put Captain Lysik and you, the crew into the Lancaster. It has more than enough flight time with the amount of fuel it carries to complete the entire mission.

The crew glanced back and forth at each other, still not sure what they had agreed to volunteer for.

"Is that all the questions you have?" queried the general and when there was no other response, he nodded to Miss Hood. She stood about five foot eight and had cropped red hair and even the uniform could not hide her perfect figure. The crew stared at the beautiful woman who was supposed to lead them in their first real mission.

"Alright gentlemen, as you are already aware, I will be known to you as Commander Hood as in Little Red Riding Hood and my friend here will be Mr. Wolf. The others are just the Big Bad Wolves. She smiled toward the three men in the first row. I have the rank of colonel and therefore while I'm with you, I will be your commanding officer." The men again glanced at each other. "We are Strategic Air Services and what we do best is to work behind the front lines. It will be your job to get us to our drop zone and then leave. The less we advertise, the better chance we have of completing our mission." She stopped, looked at each of the crew members and then nodded for the WC to pass out a sheath of papers to each of them.

"I would like you to study this mission plan for as long as you need to, taking particular notice of and memorizing your specific orders. Before you leave tonight, these must all be turned in and they will be destroyed. Captain, your flight plan will also be memorized. There must be no link to us jumping into Gottow." She stared again at each of the men and now they saw the fire in her eyes. "Are we clear on that?"

"Yes Ma'am," the crew said loudly in unison. The WC stood again.

"Alright men, you have as much time as you want to study your orders. When you've got them down, turn them in and await your escort back to your barracks." He and the generals filed out the door from the platform. Commander Hood and her wolves stayed to retrieve the papers.

xxxxxxxxxxxxxxxxxxxxxxxxxxxxxxxxxxxxxxxxxx

Captain David Lysik idled back the engines of the Lancaster as he engaged the emergency brake. Their bomber, the Blue Osprey as the crew had named it - with a picture of a blue osprey painted just under the pilot's window - was seventeenth in line for takeoff, but the mission flare had not yet been fired. In the direction that they were heading now, he caught sight of the last vestige of sunlight as it sank over the western horizon.

"One of the nicest days I've seen since I arrived in England," he said to Jack, as he double-checked some instruments. While waiting for the line to start moving, Dave allowed his mind to slide back to Julia and his new child. He wondered whether it would be a little boy or a little girl. Either way, he thought the baby would be the best in the world. He reminisced about the first time he had laid eyes on his beautiful wife and thought she was a real angel. A smile pursed his lips. As the memories played on in his mind, the warmth of her memory caused a smile to grow across his whole face. He had thought he would never fly again, partly because of his injuries, but mostly because of the crash. He had not only got to continue flying, but also, Julia had become his wife and now here he was, with the officer's rank of Captain. He let his mind wander to thoughts of his bride and their short honeymoon. Then, as he got to the part where they were saying goodbye, he realized that his eyes were glistening.

"Hey captain, how long do you expect it'll be before the flare?" It was Jack, his engineer, sitting to his right.

"The sun's down, so it should be any time now. I'd strap in, if I were you." Dave spoke into the intercom. "And the rest of you, prepare for take-off." He hadn't finished saying the words, when Billy yelled excitedly, "There it is, Cap. The red flare just arced across the end runway behind us."

"Alright boys, that's it! It shouldn't be too long before we're on deck," Dave said, as he watched the first Halifax swing out onto the runway and apply the brakes too hard, bobbing the nose and probably shaking up the crew. A bright green flare arced over the runway, the same as the red one had and the big bomber on deck roared as the big props began to slowly propel it down the runway. By the time it was less than half-way, the next Halifax pulled onto the runway and immediately went to take-off power.

Now the line was slowly advancing and in short order, the Blue Osprey - the only Lancaster in the line - was accelerating down the runway with all the inherent vibrations from the wheels. Faster and faster the big bomber cascaded and then, as if suddenly they had come to a halt, the air-frame was smooth and all the vibrations gone. The heavy metal bird was defying gravity and lifting away from the runway. Dave continued to keep the craft gaining altitude as the darkened English countryside became smaller.

They were in the air twenty minutes when Commander Hood moved to the flight deck. Dave sensed her presence as much as seeing her.

"How is my favourite SAS Commander doing?" Dave asked, as he noticed her crouched over to his right.

"We're okay. A lot more comfortable in those jump seats that the maintenance people installed than it is trying to sit against the fuselage back there. I calculate we should be coming up to the coast soon."

"Yes," Dave replied. "If you look right over there," he said, as he nodded to the center left, "you can see the glow of a city. Funny, it kind of reminds me of Regina." Dave glanced over at her and although he didn't expect her to answer, he asked anyway.

"What's so important about Gottow, that Britain's best has to jump in?" She hesitated for a few seconds, giving the indication that she wasn't about to tell him, then seemed to change her mind.

"There's intel that Jerry is working on some kind of super bomb and we need to get more information." She stared out the window into the darkness for a moment. "Have you ever heard of nuclear fission, Captain?" she asked.

"Well, I've read about it. It's way too complicated for me, but it's just a theory anyway. No one has been able to make it work." Hood turned back to him with raised eyebrows.

"Oh really? Well, I'm afraid that's no longer true. Apparently, Jerry may have found a way to split the atom." As Dave started to ask another question, the SAS agent waved her hands, palms out indicating that she had told all she intended to.

"OK, OK! I suppose you shouldn't be telling me all the deep dark secrets anyway."

"No, I shouldn't, but if you get us into Germany, hopefully we'll learn a lot more. I suppose I should go back and see if I can sleep.

"I'd hold off on the sleep until after we're past the coast. There's liable to be some serious ack-

ack and I'll be maneuvering to avoid it. After that, it'll probably quiet down unless Jerry has some night fighters patrolling."

"How long until we reach the coast?" Hood asked.

"Navigator, how long before we reach the coast?" Dave asked into the intercom.

"Should be there in less than fifteen minutes," he said, using the intercom. "Heading one zero eight, Captain."

"Thank you Navigator," Dave replied, as he gently banked the huge plane to the correct degree of direction. Hood nodded while giving Dave the thumbs up and clumsily moved back to just in front of the entrance hatch where the SAS would make their jump.

Dave continued to increase the altitude, which brought him into formation with the other bombers and then gained another few thousand feet of altitude along with them. The crew busied themselves with completing their initial checks.

"Captain, can I test the twin fifties?" Sergeant Brown asked, speaking of the twin Browning 50 caliber machine guns in the mid turret.

"Go ahead, Ron. That goes for you too, Billy." Instantly, Dave heard the staccato of the twins.

The Purple Heart Bride
Chapter 10

Crossing the coast was the first time most of the crew had ever experienced being under enemy fire. The flak from the 88 millimetre guns caused rough flying and Dave did his best to move around in the sky so as not to become an easy target. The barrage lasted for only ten minutes but felt like an eternity. The last few concussions shook the plane and then the crew settled into duties of checking over their equipment. Jack ensured that all systems were running smoothly, while George kept Dave apprised of a running plot line as to where they were and where they were heading. The others double-checked their guns and thought about what was going to happen when they got to the drop area. The night was dark and quiet and soon Dave allowed his mind to slip into musing about Julia and the baby. He tried to picture the baby in his mind's eye, but could not. The best he could visualize was Julia with a little bundle of cloth wrapped around the form of a baby. He wished he could be there instead of flying over Europe, but he realized that thousands of other allied military as well would rather be home tending to life in a simpler way. He wondered if the Germans had the same thoughts, or whether they were all a bunch of fanatics like Hitler, Goring and Himmler. Once Dave's mind returned to focus on the present, the time to their first target seemed to drag on like eternity.

George moved up behind Dave.

"Target coming up in fifteen minutes, Captain," George yelled over the din of the motors.

"Thanks navigator. You know, you could use the intercom. That's why they install them," Dave yelled back with a snicker.

"I know. I just wanted to move around a bit. Hey, there's the search lights over there," George said as he pointed to the front right.

"Some navigator. That's Lepzig. I'm hoping there won't be so many of them where we're going."

"No kidding," George said in awe as he stared at more than fifty shafts of lights waving frantically towards the heavens. George was still staring to the right when some lights came on a fair distance in front of them.

"There's *our* target George. You'd better get back to your station," Dave said as he pressed the mike to his throat. "Alright, everybody, time to put on the flak jackets and get ready for target. It should start to get bumpy in a few minutes," Dave said, with just a hint of excitement. The warning came not a minute too soon. The crew had just donned their heavy protection when the first shell exploded not more than fifty feet off the right wing sending a jolt from the concussion through the aircraft. The next shell hit the tail of a Halifax to the left. Dave watched as the aircraft - without its elevators - went into a sharp dive with a trail of heavy smoke. What concerned Dave most was the fact that no parachutes were visible.

Now all hell was breaking loose. It seemed as though the Germans were tossing more shells at them every second and neither Dave nor his crew could figure how they had managed to not get hit yet.

"I figure two minutes to target, Captain," George said, this time using the intercom.

"Bombardier, have you got it?"

"Got it, Captain."

"OK, I've slowed her down. I want a perfect hit," Dave said. He was at full flaps and seventy percent power with bomb bays open and wheels down. The big craft obeyed his command and slowed to just above stall speed.

"It's clear as a bell!" said the bombardier and then after sighting the target perfectly in the cross-hairs, yelled, "bombs away!" as he pressed the red button. Dave immediately levelled flaps and brought up the landing gear. The Lanc slowly began to gain altitude and speed as Dave banked around to a heading for the second part of their mission.

The German ground forces saw the Lancaster make the sharp bank and head away from the rest of the squadron in the direction of Britain. The German gunners thought that the craft had been damaged and would likely crash soon anyways, so they fixed their aim on the others. Although it wasn't factored into the plan, the Blue

Osprey was left alone to continue to the next target. Dave was surprised and thankful that the shelling seemed to have stopped and could only come to one alternative.

"Thank you Jesus," he said, wiping the sweat from his brow. He noticed that his hands were shaking and was again thankful when they finally stopped.

"Captain, we need to come to a heading of three zero three," George said. Dave brought the plane to the correct heading and leveled the wings.

"Thirty-eight minutes to the drop zone, Captain."

"Thank you, Navigator. I'm moving to 22000 feet. How did we do with our bomb run Bombardier?"

"Smack on target Sir. I don't think there was any collateral at all." Charles yelled now, somewhat excited. Dave smiled with pride for his crew.

"I want you all to know that you did a terrific job, but the next drop is even more important. Let's get our jumpers in the bulls-eye. I'm not expecting problems, but use your protection anyway." Dave reached altitude and then switched on the auto-pilot. "I need some soup. I think the adrenalin used up all my spare energy." Although there wasn't much room, he managed to get his thermos and poured the thick broth into the cup part of the thermos.

"Nothing like a hot drink of this soup to settle the nerves and the belly," Dave said with a smile. Jack glanced over at him.

"Yeah? Well, give me a t-bone with mushrooms and gravy and baked potatoes anytime," Jack said, as he went back to scanning the instrument gauges. "Man, I miss that, and coffee too! When I get back to Texas, the first thing I'm gonna do is build a barbecue pit and roast half a cow."

"I've got to say it does sound better than soup," Dave said, eyeing the thick liquid somewhat less affectionately.

"Good, then you're invited."

"Next time I write Julia, I'll be sure to tell her about the trip we have to take to the Lone Star State." Dave drank the last mouthful of his soup and screwed the top back on.

"Oh, oh, hold off on the letter for a bit," the engineer said with a worried tone. Dave glanced over at him.

"Talk to me Jack. What's going on?"

"We're losing oil pressure in number four engine. You can try and feather it and reduce power, but it looks like it might not hold. You might have to shut it down." Dave glanced again at the flight engineer and began feathering the number four prop. It was only a short time before several of the crew were asking what was happening.

"Everyone, I've feathered our number four engine as a precaution. The Lancaster will fly on

137

two engines if need be, so we still have lots of safety. As soon as Jack ascertains the problem and I know more, I'll let you know. Now Sergeant Brown, if you can move from your sling, please inform the colonel I need a word with her." It seemed like a long time before Colonel Hood managed to squeeze through the small openings to reach the front.

"Yes, Captain? Your Aussie sergeant said you wanted to speak to me. At least, I think that's what he was saying," she said, almost amiably.

"Yes Ma'am, We've lost number four and I'm not sure if we can get it back. We can make it back on three, but I guess it's your call. Do we carry on, or abort the mission?" She considered the situation.

"If at all possible, complete the entire mission, but at least get us into Gottow. After we jump, if you feel you can do the recon and the loss of the engine won't hinder you from getting your crew back to base safely, then by all means complete the whole mission." She smiled at Dave with warmth that he hadn't noticed before.

"Yes Ma'am, I'll do my best."

"Somehow, Captain, I know you will," she said, as she moved back to the parachutists' area. It took him a minute to analyze her comment and then he realized the colonel had just paid him a compliment. Dave turned back to Jack.

"How's it look there?"

"The pressure seems to have come back to

normal. I would suggest we drop the cargo," he thumbed toward the parachutists, "and then we can try putting it back into operation. It might have just been an airlock in the oil line or something," he said holding his hands palms out in resignation. They continued to the drop zone and the four SAS did a HALO (better known as a high altitude low opening jump). Dave didn't waste any time leaving the area as he had been ordered and soon was trying the number four engine. It seemed to hold. George came on the radio.

"Set course to 110 degrees in ten minutes. Time to target: one hour and thirty minutes. E.T.A. - 0900."

Shortly before the hour, Dave pushed the intercom mike up to his throat.

"OK guys, this is the hard one. We have to lose some altitude to get the best pictures. For a short while, we'll be sitting ducks for their anti-aircraft so we get in, get the recon photos and get out, and I want everyone in their flak jackets and helmets except for Billy. Even he wouldn't fit into his space with it on." He glanced down at Charley. "Bombardier, can you see anything yet?"

"Yeah, I see the first river and what looks like a huge military barracks about ten minutes ahead. I mean, it looks huge."

"I want you to get the pictures on the first wave, because I don't want to come back. Get ready, everybody. Unless the boys didn't show up for work today we should start getting pulverized anytime now." Dave had just turned slightly when the first shell exploded off to the left. He had the big plane at five thousand and kept it on a steady path towards Oswiecim where the Konzentrationlager (concentration camp) was located. Charles began taking pictures as the shells burst all around the plane.

"Captain, this place must have a thousand buildings," Charles said with an air of disbelief. "And I can see people in rows moving between some of the buildings. It looks like the whole place is fenced in and there's a rail line with a loading spur right up the center of the compound. Then further east, it appears there's another compound. What is this place, Captain?" Dave was trying to hold the plane straight and catch a glimpse of the place himself.

"Just roll the cameras so we can get out of here," Dave said, as they passed directly above the camp and then Dave pushed all four levers to full power and pulled back on the stick. The Lanc began to gain elevation and Dave dared to take a breath of relief.

They had reached eight thousand feet when one of the anti-aircraft batteries got lucky and the Osprey's luck ran out. The shell hit the number four engine, blasting it right out of its wing placement. Somehow the wing remained intact but the ailerons on that wing were fused in the neutral position. Now Dave had very little control over the aircraft except maybe to keep it airborne until everyone could jump and parachute to the ground. The chilling thought went through his mind that it might turn out his crew would be in that Konzentrationlager.

"Alright everybody, prepare to jump. I'll hold the controls as long as I can. May the Lord be with you… get going." Dave glanced at the altimeter which showed they were already down to 6000 feet and losing about one hundred feet a minute. Charles threw Dave the film canister and saluted before exiting from the hatch at the rear of the front bubble. The others left the plane through the side hatch slightly behind Sergeant Brown's station. Dave held the Lancaster as stable as he could while he double-checked to ensure that he had done everything that was necessary and tried to figure approximately where they were. They had been moving west by southwest so he supposed they were somewhere across the Polish-Czechoslovak border.

Makes little difference, he thought. *It's all Nazi controlled territory anyway.*

Chapter 11
The Purple Heart Bride

Dave stuffed the canister in one of the inside pockets of his jacket and set the plane on autopilot before making his way to the same hatch that Charles and Jack had exited. One quick glance back at the interior of the Osprey and then Dave tumbled out the hatch into a free-fall. It seemed as though he would crash into the earth by the time he counted to ten and then pulled the ripcord, to be jolted suddenly to a slower decent. Dave jerked around until he found his plane and then watched as it became smaller and smaller, until it looked like a small sliver. Then suddenly - as it met the horizon - a huge fireball mushroomed and the Osprey was only a memory. Minutes later, Dave hit the ground with his heels and tumbled in textbook fashion as the parachute school had taught him.

He landed at the edge of a field and quickly gathered his 'chute, ran into a wooded area and covered it with brush. In a crouched position, inside the tree line, he tried to orient himself. He checked the direction of the sun and began moving toward it, thinking his crew would have landed in an easterly line. Twenty minutes later, he saw Jack and then Charles. They had spotted him also, and hurried towards their captain. They continued eastward and met up with Ron and Billy.

"Didn't you guys see where George and Terry

came down?" Dave asked as they all crouched in the safety of the thick trees. The three couldn't make eye contact with Dave.

"They didn't make it, mate," Ron said quietly. "George's chute didn't open and Terry broke his neck falling from a tree. We thought it best to bury them and hide their parachutes." Dave could see that the men were deeply hurt by the loss of their fellow crew members as was he, himself - after all, he had grown up with George - but although he had a difficult time dealing with his emotions, he knew he had to stay strong for his men.

"Sir, do you think it would be right to say a few words for them - like a prayer or a eulogy or something?" Billy asked, as if he had read Dave's mind. Dave nodded, made a gesture for all of them to gather around and bowed his head.

"Lord, George was my best friend and never failed to follow you as he knew it. I don't know where Terry's faith was at, but he was a cheerful man and he gave his life fighting the evil of Nazism. We commit them to you Lord and hope that you will find them a place in your kingdom. Amen." They all said amen and raised their heads, with their eyes wet with tears. Dave gazed toward heaven and silently added a short appendage. *"Lord would you watch out for the rest of us and send those heathen Nazis to hell. Amen."* Dave glanced at the men. He could see that their spirits were low, but he knew they couldn't stay here too long because the

Wehrmacht, and probably the SS would be searching for them.

"Men, we'll have a few minutes' rest here and then we'll move out," he said, feeling proud that he had made the decision.

"Yeah, but in which direction?" Charles asked. "If we head toward home, we have to cross Germany. East or North and we go through Poland. South is Austria. Any direction we take is in German control." Everyone was perplexed and it showed on their faces. Several times one or the other began to put an idea into words and then realized the danger in heading in that direction.

Suddenly they became aware of the rifles that had come seemingly out of nowhere and were leveled at them. Dave stared down the barrel of a Luger held by a man who showed, by his flint-like gaze, that one move would be Dave's last. The others were equally solemn, and armed with rifles. The soldier with the Luger seemed to be in charge and he motioned with the barrel of the pistol for Dave to raise his hands. The crew was directed to raise theirs as well.

Dave noticed that these men were not Wehrmacht or SS, but rather a tattered group, half in uniformed khaki and half in civilian clothes. Dave thought they might be a resistance group. However, because these men could be a citizen's militia who could choose to execute the crew on the spot and then report to the authorities, he would hold off on rejoicing.

"Where do you come from, Englais, Amarica?" the man with the Luger asked in broken English.

"We are from Canada… All of us," Dave replied and noticed a slight relaxation in the leaders eyes.

"That was your plane over Oswiecim this morning."

"Yes."

"You were going to bomb the camp and then thought better of it?"

"No, it was a reconnaissance mission." Dave decided to not mention the film yet. "Who are you?" The leader's face hinted at a smile.

"I am Joseph and this is some of our Czechoslovakian resistance army. We will try to get you all out of here, alive, but for now we must move from here. The Nazis will soon be swarming this area." Joseph gave orders to his band of which - Dave now noticed - two were women. He sent half his band across the nearby field and when they had disappeared into the trees, he waved for Dave, the crew and the rest of his army to follow him in what Dave figured was a westerly direction.

Both groups reached the resistance army's camp at last light. It was comprised of about fifty lean-tos spread out through a large area of the forest. Dave noticed the sentries as he and his crew made their way towards the heart of the camp. Joseph pointed to what appeared to be an abandoned lean-to.

"You and your crew will use that one. Our comrades who used it were captured yesterday and probably shot shortly afterwards." Joseph stood quiet with a solemn stare at the small abode. "Barak was one of our best men. He and his small group supplied many of the weapons for this army by raiding Nazi out-posts," he said with a sad voice. He held the mood for several minutes and then lightened.

"I know they fought valiantly before being overcome. Milan there will show you around and get you some supper." Joseph wheeled and headed off toward another part of the camp.

Milan stood five foot ten inches and weighed in at near 195 pounds. He had the physique of a weightlifter, but moved with the spryness of a deer. He showed the Canadians the camp and then sat down with them near the soup kitchen to eat supper.

"Do you fly all the way from Canada in your aeroplane?" he asked between gulps of his soup. Dave smiled.

"No we flew out of England. Even so, it took a few hours to get here," Dave said honestly, as he decided to ask a few of his own questions.

"Have you been with this army long?" Dave asked.

"Six months. I was being arrested when Joseph's army raided the outpost I was being held at. They rescued me and I joined the group. There are many small groups who raid Nazi convoys and compounds. We also attack known Nazi informants. They are the worst." Milan went silent for a while as if recalling some of their raids. "What do you do back in Canada?"

"I help my parents on the farm and I just finished two years of college." Dave answered wistfully.

"I'm afraid most of us are not so well educated, but most here know much about farming and now we know much about the art of war." Joseph said as he stepped up behind Dave.

"What was this *reconnaissance* you were doing over Oswiecim?" he asked.

"We were getting pictures from the air," he said as he pulled out the small canister with the film in it to show them. "I need to get back to England and get these developed so that our people can try to figure out what that huge compound is. I don't suppose you know do you?" Dave asked. Joseph's face and that of all the others who were within earshot, suddenly went cold and hard. He was silent for a long minute and then stared Dave in the eye.

"The Germans call it KL Auschwitz. The KL stands for Konzentration Lager (Concentration camp), but it is really an extermination camp. They transport Jews, Gypsy, Checks, and other, ah, undesirables, using their terms, there. They remove anything of value, work them as long as the person is physically useful and then gas them. The bodies are then burned in the crematoriums. My family and many of the families and friends of these people," he spread his hand around to his ragtag army, "have been murdered there. We have knowledge of several more of these kinds of camps, but this is the closest." He sat as if trying to deal with the hurt. "Who knows how many there are." Dave was overwhelmed with this information.

"So this is how you fight against them? I mean you raid outposts and convoys to get revenge?" Dave asked.

"It's more than revenge. It's about a whole life system - our faith, our beliefs. We and many others will continue to battle them until we have no more breath. Or we defeat them. The fact is we have a raiding party leaving within the hour. Maybe you would like to come along as an observer this time? You and your men will join us, yes?" he asked. Dave glanced at his crew who nodded back.

"Yeah, I guess if you'll have us we'll join, but we don't know much about this kind of fighting." Joseph leaned closer to Dave with a face seemingly set in flint.

"Not much to know. Kill the enemy. Do as much damage to the enemy as possible and don't get killed," he said with a solemn look that made a shiver go up Dave's neck.

Joseph suggested that Dave leave the film at camp, just in case they were captured and Dave reluctantly gave the small container to Milan, who said he would have one of his men guard it with his life.

Two hours later, Joseph's army was encircling a small town. Joseph smiled at Dave and nodded toward the town.

"There is an outpost here with a radio transmitter. There is also an armoury for a detachment of the police who work with the Nazis."

"What's the name of the town?" Dave asked.

"Skripov. We will quietly overwhelm the outpost, retrieve as many small arms as we can and take the transmitter. Your crew is in good hands with Milan who will attack from the other side of town. Now, no more talking and stay with me," he whispered as he instantly stood in a crouch and ran stealthily to the end of the main street. Dave could see the brick building with a Wehrmacht truck sitting in front. The tower was on the roof and stood forty feet high. Dave stayed within a few feet of Joseph as the leader of the group silently progressed toward the building. They were within thirty feet of the door when Dave caught a glimpse of Milan and his group moving cautiously from the opposite end of town.

One of Joseph's men reached the doorway and was standing beside the entrance with his back against the wall, when a SS soldier came out the door to get some air. The man swiftly brought the butt of his rifle around catching the SS officer by surprise while busting his nose, jaw and many teeth and knocking him onto his back. The bayonet pierced the Nazi's throat and spinal cord before he even hit the ground. The commotion alerted those inside, but before they could react properly, Joseph and the rest of his men burst in, spraying the rooms with machine gun fire. The minute it took to sweep the building seemed to take forever to Dave, who could only watch with his own sidearm drawn. As the staccato of the shooting ended, Joseph found a crowbar and ripped off the door latch to the armory. There - before their eyes - were machine guns, dozens of rifles, German grenades and boxes of explosive. Quickly, Joseph organized his people to carry what they could and withdraw to the forest.

Milan had unhooked the transmitter and left with his group. Joseph and Dave were just leaving the building as a German Wehrmacht truck filled with soldiers sped down the street from the direction Milan's group had retreated. Some of the soldiers had already jumped off and were in hot pursuit of Milan's group. Joseph with four machine guns slung over his shoulder let blast at the truck with a fifth gun. The truck lights were smashed out immediately and it came to a halt with steam spewing from the radiator. The remainder of soldiers in the back jumped out and filed to either side on the run. All was chaos as Dave heard shots from Milan's direction. He glanced around in an instant and not being able to find Joseph, turned to run to where he figured

Joseph had gone. Dave had only taken a few steps when he felt the hard butt of a rifle smash against the back of his head. He crashed face first into the ground. When he regained consciousness, he felt the soldier's boot on the small of his back and the barrel pressing a little higher. Joseph had told him that to be captured by the Wehrmacht was generally better than the SS and as Dave turned to gaze at the soldier he recognized the patches. These were Wehrmacht.

The soldier roughly raised Dave to his feet and pushed and prodded him over to their truck. He made Dave climb into the back of the truck and directed him to sit. Dave reached his hand back and felt the swelling on the back of his head as it ached with a pain worse than he had ever felt before. When he looked at his hand it was covered with blood. As his vision adjusted more he saw several other soldiers drag four bodies up the street. He recognized three; two from the camp, and Ron. They were all dead, but Jack, Charley and Billy must have got away. It was a bittersweet moment. He was happy that three were still free and alive, yet sad that the sergeant had been killed. He would always remember him.

In the early shades of morning light, five soldiers climbed into the back of the truck and the driver made a U-turn heading north and left in the direction from which it had come. The truck had rumbled on for hours when one of the guards offered Dave a cigarette. Rather than risk upsetting him, Dave accepted and the guard lit it.

"Do you know where you are taking me?" Dave asked as he cautiously blew out the smoke.

"Ja," one of the soldiers said. "Ve haf orders to take you to Gestapo headquarters in Dresdan. You vill probably wished we had shot you like your friends." Dave didn't ask any more questions as his mind dwelt on what Joseph had told him. "The Gestapo can make you want to tell them everything you know."

It was afternoon by the time Dave arrived at Gestapo headquarters and as he was marched in, he expected the worst. He was glad that he had given the canister to Milan now because he was sure he wouldn't be able to deliver it. He was marched into an office. The man behind the desk was a large man, but his size wasn't wasted on fat.

"Captain Lysik, I hope your ride here was not too uncomfortable. It's the war, you see and the higher ups,,, well they requisition the best transportation." The man said all this with a smirk and then his face went sullen. "How did an, let's see here, oh please sit down." He shuffled some papers around. "Ah yes, a Royal Canadian Air Force captain get picked up with a group of murderers? How does that happen Herr Lysik?" The man looked at the papers again. "Lysik, is that a Jewish name?" He nodded at the SS officer standing beside Dave. Instantly a baton crashed down on Dave's skull.

"Ah," Dave gasped. "Canadian, I was born north of Prince Albert, Saskatchewan, Cana-" The man cut him off as he nodded again and this time the baton smashed across his face.

"I have your file Jew boy! What I need to know is what you were doing over Auschwitz. And you will tell me." Again another nod and another smashing blow that sent Dave onto the floor. Dave rose from the floor as if he was about to stand and then decided not to and fell back into the chair. His entire face was now a mat of blood and he could barely see.

"We were on a reconnaissance mission to get pictures of the camp," Dave said just above a mumble. He hoped that by volunteering the information it might steer them away from the more delicate part.

"And where is this film?" the man questioned. He nodded, and the baton hit him again, with like results.

"They were lost with the plane. Didn't have time to retrieve it before jumping," Dave managed to say, almost passing out. Dave didn't think the Gestapo agent believed the story until the man picked up his knee board. His mission excluding the SAS jump was all detailed there.

"You've been a busy little Jew boy. It says here your mission was to bomb a German city and perform a reconnaissance of a Reich facility. Of course you know that is espionage,-- punishable by death. No matter, I think we have all we want. I think I have the perfect place for you. Have this man transferred to our relocation camp at Treblinka. They will teach him that Jews don't bomb our cities or take pictures of our facilities.

The Purple Heart Bride
Chapter 12

Dave was escorted to the train station where he was put into the last car of the train - a passenger rail car with two guards. They were the only occupants and Dave began to realize that something was seriously wrong with this situation. He had caught a glimpse of the other rolling stock of the train and they were cattle cars, except they weren't filled with cattle, but rather people. They were old, young, men, women, boys, girls and even babies. He could only surmise that what Joseph had told him was true and these people were also on their way to one of the camps - even babies? He had also noticed that they had a sad look about them. Their eyes didn't have any sparkle, nor did they seem full of fear, as he would have expected, but rather were tired or even dead to emotion. He couldn't understand the expression and he thought about it for many hours as the train rumbled east.

Dave watched the towns as they passed without stopping or even slowing down and wondered where this awful train was headed. He knew that they must be halfway across Poland by now, but had no idea what the destination was, except apparently to a 'relocation camp' at a town called Treblinka. Dave had never heard of the place.

Suddenly the train started lurching and slowing. As Dave peered out the small window, he saw the rail sign, and read "Warsaw". The train finally came to a jerking halt, almost causing him and the two guards to be thrown off the seats. The guards stood and motioned for Dave to get off the train in front of them. He realized that he was being allowed to stretch his legs.

He again noticed the other cars and saw that those people were not being allowed off. Instead, he saw that men were going to each car and grabbing buckets that were so completely full that they sloshed over the top. One of the men passed Dave with a bucket and the stench from it almost sickened him. These were what the people had to use as toilets. A bucket of water was brought back for each car and, because it looked exactly the same as the one that had been taken away, Dave couldn't help wondering if it was indeed the same one. The whole operation took less than fifteen minutes and then Dave was prodded back into the passenger rail car. Soon the train was moving full speed down the track again.

The train was still headed in an easterly direction and Dave wondered if maybe these people and he were being delivered to Russia. Maybe all the horror stories were just that - stories. Maybe these people were being relocated to the forests of western Russia. However, the treatment of those in the cattle cars didn't correspond with that idea. The train rumbled on.

Dave had fallen asleep sometime during the

night and was awakened by the shrill warning horn of the locomotive. He found it difficult to open his eyes because of the swelling, but finally was able to see that it was daylight and the train was slowing down. Through the small window, he could see that the train was approaching a siding where a wooden ramp had been built and all the cars were just inside a high wire gate, when the train came to a sudden halt. He could read a large sign in German over the doorway of what looked like a railway station, "Relocation Camp."

The guards prodded him with their rifles to move off the train. He stepped down onto the ramp and it was then he noticed that, unlike the two soldiers that had been guarding him, the ones here had the two lightning bolts of the SS on their uniform.

Dave gazed around him and realized that there must have been a thousand people, mostly Jews, on this train. The camp, or at least what he could see of it, looked to be on a chunk of land about the size of his parents' farm, with nearly a quarter of it covered by wooden barracks. He saw some other buildings beyond some trees, which were larger, but had no idea what they were for.

The commandant walked briskly over to Dave. The officer stared at him with a fiendish smile and nodded to two other SS officers who were on either side of him.

"So you are the Canadian Jew boy who has bombed our cities," he said, with a sneer in his voice. "Take this vermin to his barracks and *explain* to him how things work around here." Dave especially didn't like the way he had drawn out the word explain.

With one officer on each side, they pushed, kicked and shoved him through the terminal building, through an open compound and finally to a row of buildings. They shoved him into one of them and began beating him. Dave was almost unconscious when the SS decided that his orientation was complete and they just left. He gazed around the structure and at first thought it was a cattle barn and the bins on either side of the building were stanchions, but since they were stacked three high, he realized that the bins were very large and rough bunk beds. Momentarily, he fearfully wondered what he had gotten himself into. It was then that a small voice inside him said, "I will never leave thee or forsake thee." It was Hebrews 13:5, and Dave remembered the next verse as well: "So that we may boldly say, the Lord is my Helper, and I will not fear what man shall do unto me." Dave immediately prayed that the Lord would spare him and keep him from further beatings. It helped calm his fear, but he was still hurting badly.

As Dave studied the long, narrow, dirty building, a large man with an arm band that had KAPO on it entered the building. He didn't seem to have the contempt that the SS had, nor did he show any sympathy. With a baton at the ready, he took Dave to a building that was a type of bath house without baths and let him clean up. He told Dave to be ready for work the next morning and to return to the barrack building as soon as he was cleaned up. The big man then turned and left.

Dave could see a somewhat distorted image of himself in a shiny piece of tin that someone had set in front of the wash trough. The image was distorted in the shiny metal, but even more grotesque due to the swelling and the wounds. He gingerly dabbed his face around the many wounds to try and clean the dried blood away. As he was finishing up, another man entered. Dave had never seen anyone so thin. It was if the man had only a sheet of skin over his skeleton and Dave was surprised when the man spoke.

"I saw the SS work you over," he said, as he inspected Dave's injuries. Do you have any other wounds?"

"I feel like I just went 9 rounds with Jack Dempsey. There isn't an inch of my body that doesn't ache." At this the fellow inmate smiled.

"These SS aren't here just to keep us inside the camp. They mean to kill us – sooner or later. So you come from Canada?"

"Yeah, I was shot down over Oswiem and captured with a Czech resistance group."

"You are fortunate to have even made it this far, but I fear unless a miracle happens, this is the end of the road for all of us. My name is Azrial

161

Barak. I'm the closest thing we have here to a doctor. I had a large practice in Berlin before the war but I think my work here is even more important. The SS don't allow me any clinic or medicines." His eyes drooped further as his thoughts seemed to go other places. Finally, he perked up a bit. "I do what I can to ease some of the suffering. So what is your name?"

"I'm Dave Lysik." Dave winced as the doctor dabbed once more on one of the wounds.

He looked Dave over one more time and then shook his head.

"If you keep out of their way, David, you might survive for a while."

xxxxxxxxxxxxxxxxxxxxxxxxxxxxxxxxxxxxxxxxxxx

Only a week had passed since Dave had arrived in this place that would have rivaled Dante's Inferno, except for the fact this was real, and he was already acutely aware that the SS had an entirely unique definition of relocation. Their treatment was one of disdain and hatred toward this people whom they implied murdered Jesus. Dave also had no misgivings that if these Nazis had their way, whatever his reward might be in the hereafter, he would soon be collecting.

Dave, as a born again Christian and believing that God answered prayer, was not so sure that his prayer to be spared in the daily selections was a blessing, after receiving his task to recover the booty from the corpses. His grotesque job was, to

162

him, more macabre than any other activity in the camp, including the murder of these poor people. Searching and removing all valuables from the corpses, with the sentence of instant death if he missed anything, made him sick to his stomach. He tried to send his mind to other places while he performed the objectionable tasks, but it was useless. He even considered just refusing and accept death. Somehow, this seemed a coward's way out though, so he continued. The bile was always moving up in his throat as he searched in forbidden places for the gold fillings, jewelry or money the Nazi pigs coveted.

Dave searched the faces of the people who worked around him. He learned the stories of a few whom he was able to talk with. He heard many gruesome stories of arrests, torture, fiendish treatment and even murder . For them, the rise of Nazism meant the continual progression of oppression of the Jewish people of Europe. Everything had gradually been taken away from them, both physically and spiritually, until they were reduced to empty shells. Many had died in transit and many more in the work camps before the remainder had their right to live revoked in the SS death camps like this one. There were a few whose spirits would not be broken, but, all too often, these would be shot outright.

Dave - a Canadian pilot - on the other hand, could very well have been shot as a spy, but the

Germans, hitting upon his Jewish background, didn't really care about his story. It was disconcerting to them to have to admit that a Jew could actually bomb the Fatherland and they wanted to exact some revenge. Now, however, it appeared that this camp was the end of the line for him.

Dave stared up at the dark rough lumber of the bunk above him with his darker, solemn thoughts somewhere between consciousness and sleep. Sometimes he prayed, sometimes he thought of Julia, home and his young son.

The days slowly blended into weeks and then months, but every morning the silence was shattered once again by the Kapos banging their batons on the dividers between the bunks. As Dave gazed over the nine or ten men that slept in each bunk, most would be rousted out and onto the cold wood floor. Each morning, Dave saw that several didn't move and he watched as the special Komandos would remove their corpses. As Dave raised his eyelids with the prison horns blaring, a Kapo's baton smashed the wood, with a loud crack, just above his head.

"Get up you lazy scum. It's 4:00 A.M. There's lots of work to do and it'll be your death if you don't get up and get moving."

Everyone who was alive was moving to the compound for roll call and had to stand until the vile SS officers allowed them to get their meager morning rations.

"Do they have to do this every bloody morning?" Dave asked no one in particular as he stood, freezing cold.

"Don't worry, it's not much longer. Your life expectancy here is not much more than six months. If they can't work you to death by that time, you're not much use to them and--," he ran his finger across his throat. "—you've had it. When they move you into the chute," the man said as he nodded to a gate on the southwest corner of the compound, "you're finished. I'm already running on a prayer. I've been here a few months, so it won't be long for me. What ghetto did you come from?"

Dave turned with a start. He could speak fluent German, but this man was speaking English. As he focused on the man, he realized that this frail creature beside him was the robust fellow who had eaten soup that evening at Joseph's camp.

"Milan, is that you? By God, it is you! Were you captured the same night as me? We were told that you were shot." The man didn't seem to recognize him.

"I'm David - David Lysik. Don't you remember me? I'm the Canadian. I was captured during the raid with Joseph's Partisan's group. I still can't figure how I didn't get shot." The man, Milan, leaned closer.

"Quiet, you fool, or they'll just shoot us here and now."

The men all lined up and the camp

commandant began speaking, giving an ultimatum of work or death and then casually walked off to his quarters. Another SS officer ordered the Polish guards and Komandos to escort the ones whose names were called out, to a special detail. Milan leaned closer to Dave.

"Special work detail, yeah, yeah. It's a special detail alright - to be gassed." Milan said.

"B640346, R453267 and G975213." The officer said as he read a list of numbers.

"Oh my God, G975213 - that's my number," Milan said in a trembling voice. "Looks like my prayers didn't work this time." He leaned closer. "Before I go, I'll give you these back," and he slipped two small aluminum canisters into Dave's hand. "The one is your pictures and the other is very classified intelligence and I'll tell you two things. Find Abraham. When you find him you'll know why. Second, if you can, get this information to the Allies. Before this mess, I was a highly paid physicist and worked in a very secret complex. Hitler is very close to building a very powerful bomb. If you can reach American Lt. Colonel, George Baker, use the password: 'The harvest is ready." He will ask, 'do you think you have enough?" and you reply, 'My cup is running over.' If you're sent to the gas, try to pass the information on."

The Kapo swung his baton, narrowly missing Dave and it hit Milan on the side of the head. The emaciated Jewish Czech yelped as he stumbled, but didn't completely fall. The Kapo pointed with his baton.

"Get moving," he yelled as he herded Milan away.

Late that night in his bunk, Dave slipped the second canister out and carefully looked at its contents. He could make out some maps, a large building and some complicated equations. Although he knew little of what the equations alluded to, he did recognize the heading 'Fission Bomb'. Milan was right; this was very important. He put the canister away and prayed.

"Lord, show me a way out of this hell and numb my senses to this horror while I'm in it." A voice from across the bunk quietly said, "Amen."

The next morning, Dave began his search for Abraham, but no one seemed to know anyone in the camp by that name. It wasn't until many days had passed, that a tall, slender man began working near Dave and when the opportunity came, moved in close.

"I'm wondering why you're searching for Abraham?"

"A friend of mine told me to find him, but only told me I'd know him when I found him," Dave replied.

"That's because Abraham isn't a man - it's an operation, a plan. You'll be contacted," he said and then headed for the SS guard with a small bucket of gold teeth.

Those words rolled over and over in Dave's

mind. What kind of operation could these poor broken men possibly carry out? After all, they were barely capable of continued breathing. He finished the day with a bowl of cabbage soup that was very light on the cabbage and then he collapsed into the bunk. Sometime later in the night, he was awakened by being shaken and then hit in the face with a rifle butt. He shrieked in agony as blood spurted from his face. Two Polish guards drug him out of the barracks and across the compound to the commandant's office. They plunked him into a chair in the center of the room.

"Do you know why you're here?" Dave shook his head.

I wouldn't tell you if I did, he thought. "No." he finally said. This resulted in a baton whacking the side of the head, and he nearly passed out.

"We know about the escape plan and we want to know when, where and how you plan to do it." The officer had a smirk on his face. "Why don't you make it easy on yourself and tell us who this Abraham is." Suddenly, he realized that they were just fishing and had very little knowledge of the operation.

"I don't know any Abraham," he said, as convincingly as possible. The commandant nodded to the two guards, who began to beat him with their batons, as well as kick him. The beatings and questions continued until Dave was an unconscious, bloody mess on the floor.

When Dave awoke to the sirens in the morning,

there wasn't a square inch of his body that didn't scream out in pain. He tried to move, but his limbs were sluggish. He knew from stories he'd heard that if you went to the infirmary, your next stop was the gas chamber, so he struggled to get his limbs moving, even though every movement caused searing pain. It was a struggle, but by the time he was to start work, he could move fairly well.

Weeks passed, giving Dave's wounds a chance to begin healing. He was in the Kanada building, performing his ghastly task, when the Kapo whom he had first seen when he arrived, sidled up to him.

"A meeting tonight at the end of the barracks," he said out the side of his mouth and then, without missing a beat, he started yelling, cursing and threatening before moving down the line.

That night, Dave crept down to the end of the barracks and was surprised to find twenty-five men quietly conversing. When they saw the young Canadian, they smiled and greeted him. The leader of the group shook his hand. "Choice greetings, Lysik; we are very sorry for the beating you received." Dave scanned the group and leaned in as if to tell a secret.

"You must be very careful. The Nazis know of your plan. There must be a spy in your group," Dave said cautiously.

"There *was* a spy in our group. If you look over there between the bunks you'll see the feet of poor Danyal. Poor fellow tripped and broke his neck." The muscular leader continued. "We weren't sure if they had planted you, him or both so we gave you each a different piece of information about Abraham and when you came back looking like you just ran headfirst into the last train, we knew he was the plant." He gave Dave a minute to digest what he had just said and then sat down. Dave stared at the large muscular man.

"Anyway my name is Mitzak," he said, as he introduced the others. "Abraham is the name of our operation and is a plan to escape. It is on for next month and we could use your help."

"Wait a minute. What do you figure you're going to fight them with, sticks? You don't have any weapons." The leader chuckled and then caught himself.

"Now that's true, and we were going to buy some, but Danyal there got the information and leaked it to the SS. Our man with the money was shot and the money confiscated. So we don't have any weapons, but they do, in the armory and we've got a key to it." He nodded to a man in the group. "John's family manufactured those locks before the war and with the serial number from the lock, he duplicated a key yesterday. I'd say we should have quite an arsenal." Dave was beginning to think that escape might be possible, after all.

"There is one thing you should know," Dave

said. "I have been given a very important secret from a fellow named Milan, just before he went to the gas and I think the SS know it's here somewhere. This material must get to the Allies." Mitzak looked at the others before turning back to Dave.

"What is this important secret?" he asked.

"It's maps, blueprints and equations. It sounds as if Hitler is close to building a fission bomb. I also have a spool of aerial photos of Auschwitz." Dave could see by the look on their faces that they had never heard the term 'fission'. "I've heard in theory the bomb could level a city the size of Warsaw. If we can get the information to the Allies, they might be able to destroy it before Hitler can use it and that might shorten the war.

Mitzak glanced at each of his friends and then turned to Dave.

"I would say then your escape is a top priority. Hmm maybe we could provide a smokescreen to make sure you make it." He eyed Dave up and down with a grin on his face. "In fact, I think I might have an idea how we can beat the SS at their own game. What if, after we enter the armory and get the weapons, we relieve the first SS about your size of his uniform?" Mitzak had a broad smile now. "If we make it out the gate, you can act as if you're chasing us shooting just over our heads. If you stay close enough after us, the guards won't shoot for fear of hitting one of their own and it's good for everyone. When we get past the tree line, we scatter. You, Dave, can circle north and then east. The rest of us will go the other way. I think we have a good possibility of success." Finally, Mitzak motioned for Dave to sit down and join in the final plans. Mitzak leaned forward and spoke in hushed tones.

"On the morning of the escape, we head for our jobs as usual, but any who can will divert and stop by the armory where they will get their weapons. As soon as we suit up Dave, we will attack the guard tower by the gate. Once the tower is disabled, we place explosives under the gate and blow it out of the way. Others will charge the commandant's office and the SS barracks. Anyone who doesn't have a weapon will set fire to the buildings. After we detonate the gate, we will cut through the outer perimeter wire and run for the trees with Dave chasing and shooting in our direction." He made eye contact with each of the conspirators and nodded his head. "Okay, inform your groups of the plan and be ready to go. We'll pass the code word Abraham when it's time; then we'll meet at the armory the next morning," he said with finality.

Dave returned to his bunk and thought about the plan.

"It had promise," he thought, "but it would take a miracle to actually pull it off." It was then that he heard a very calm, gentle voice in his spirit that almost scared him.

"Fear not. Only believe."

"Sometimes easier said than done," he thought. Dave mulled this over and over again in his mind until sleep overcame him. He would consider this biblical command many times over the next days while waiting for the code name Abraham which would signal that the plan was about to happen. Also, during this time he was beaten several times most severely, to the point Dave began to think he may not live to hear that code word.

It was now the middle of July 1944. Although the camp was in an open space surrounded by trees, it was still very hot in the compound. Dave was performing the same gruesome task he had been assigned to when he first arrived, but still could not, and would not, let himself get used to it. As he began searching a corpse, a kapo yelled at him to speed up and when Dave turned about to tell him to go to hell, he saw that it was the large Kapo who helped him when he had first arrived. Nevertheless, he was so fed up, he threw his hands up.

"Go to hell, you big ape!" he said loudly. He saw the big man give a slight grin just before he hit Dave with his baton. The pain made Dave sink to his knees as the man stood over him, pelting him with more, less severe blows. Dave felt like he was about to pass out. The man bent down closer to him.

"You stupid Jew," the Kapo said in a loud voice. "If you were truly Abraham's son, you would understand the name, *Abraham!* Now get back to work!" With one hand, he jerked Dave back onto his feet. It hit Dave almost immediately. The code word! The plan would go forward tomorrow morning. He did his task the rest of the day, thinking only of the plan.

The next morning, Dave was awake before the horns blared and felt exceptionally well, considering all the beatings he had received. When roll call was done, he finished his breakfast and headed toward his job that would take him directly past the armoury. As he was approaching the munitions building, a hand grabbed him by the collar. It was SS Sergeant Von Hickel.

"And where do you think you're going, scum?" Von Hickel said in a gruff voice. A fleeting thought passed through Dave's mind that this man was almost his exact size and the thought "this could be the uniform I get to wear" almost made him smile. Suddenly returning to reality, he was not sure whether any of the others had made it inside the armory or not. He decided to try and become a diversion without becoming a corpse. He stumbled and then regaining his balance, moved in an arc, so Von Hickel's back was to the building's door.

"I'm just going to my job," Dave said, as he recovered his balance and nodded in the direction of the Kanada building.

"Well, you had better move a whole lot faster or, oh hell, why don't I just shoot you right now and be done with you." Von Hickel growled as reached for his side arm. A bicep of the muscular Mitzak came silently from behind. His arm wrapped around the evil man's neck very quickly and with a violent jerk, there was the sound of the neck snapping. The sergeant went limp and would never shoot anyone again.

"Hurry up, help me get him inside," Mitzak barked. "Looks like we've got your uniform."

As Dave donned the sergeant's uniform, more than 150 prisoners filed through, arming themselves with all manner of German military weapons. Everything was proceeding like clockwork until another SS officer stumbled on the activity. He was about to alert his comrades when a bullet silenced him and did the job for him. Now all was chaos. The horns were blaring and guards were shooting from the towers.

A few of the prisoners sprayed the closest tower with machine gun fire and finally killed the two guards in it. During this time, a squad of prisoners planted nitro-glycerine under the gate. All but one was shot before they could clear the area. Mitzak sized up the situation and decided that the gate had to go immediately. He took aim and squeezed the trigger. The blast knocked him down and when he had scrambled to his feet, he saw the crater where the gate had once been. He then realized that they had used twenty times the amount needed to do the job. The closest guard tower was also blown to pieces and a nearby building was missing a corner with the roof sagging down, and it was also ablaze.

"Run! Run! Remember the plan," Mitzak screamed as he waved his arms to follow him. Suddenly a flood of hundreds of prisoners surged through the crater and in the smoke and confusion, many were able to make it to the outside perimeter wire. It was then that a second tower, although somewhat distant, opened up and many of the prisoners were cut down. Mitzak and others worked feverishly to cut the wire of the outer perimeter and soon the remaining prisoners were flooding out onto the open field. Dave charged after them, screaming incoherently and shooting just over their heads. The ruse worked perfectly. The men in the tower held their fire, not wanting to hit an SS sergeant. They not only didn't shoot Dave, but didn't even shoot in the direction of the prisoners. More than eighty prisoners escaped with their lives.

As soon as Dave was past the tree line and out of the tower's sight, he holstered his sidearm and began a wide arc to the right around the camp. By evening, he was twenty kilometres northeast of the camp and about ten kilometres south of Bialystok. He was just about to leave the narrow road when he spied a group of young SS soldiers driving toward him in a Schwimmwagon. He had heard the Germans had a car that would float across rivers or lakes while being moved along by a small propeller. This was the first time that he had seen the innovative craft. His only option was to continue down the road towards them. They came to a stop near the sergeant and asked what he was doing away out here. Dave ascertained that there were four of them and stepped closer to the vehicle.

"I was out here searching for you four," he said as authoritatively as he could, "where the hell have you been?"

We finished burying the fuhrer's train and then stopped at a guesthouse for some snaps. We were told that was allowed." Dave wondered what they meant by that, but tried to put on a show that he was suspicious as he sidled up to the driver's window. When he reached an area where they couldn't see his right hand, he drew his sidearm. With an aim that he had practised in training, he quickly raised the Luger and shot all four of the officers. Dave wrestled the driver over onto another soldier in the passenger seat and headed cross country, thinking he now had the means to reach Russia or close to it. He travelled until he was out of sight of the road and then dumped the bodies in a small thicket.

He travelled for what seemed forever, cutting around woodlots and crossing fields and finally came to a river. Dave now had the chance to try out this German engineering marvel. He got it into the water quite easily, using a place that probably was used for gathering water, so the slope was nearly level on entrance. However, after he got the prop working and slowly crossed the river, the vehicle got bogged down while he was trying to get out on the other side. He left the machine and carried on by foot.

He hadn't hiked very far, when he came upon a treed area. It was dusk now and he was very tired, so he found what he thought would be a safe place, sitting with his back against the trunk of a tree and settled in for a rest. He was soon fast asleep.

It was a gray light before dawn when he was awakened by the cold steel of a gun barrel nudging at his temple.

"*Now I've had it,*" he thought. The man with the rifle pressed it a little harder against the side of his head.

"You filthy, miserable, Nazi pig. Stand up before I shoot you where you sit," the man growled. As Dave stood, he could see ten others a few meters away. He suspected that they were Partisans and a dread thought suddenly hit Dave. He was wearing the uniform of their most hated enemy.

"Comrade," he blurted out. "I used this uniform to escape. The officer who owned it is now dead. Look at the trousers. They are too long and look at my left arm. See?" He pulled up the sleeve to display a six digit number. "The swine tattooed a number there." He unbuttoned the tunic. "See the filthy rags which are my own clothes? I am not a German - I am a Canadian pilot. I was shot down after a reconnaissance mission." The group leader checked each detail, then smiled and grasped Dave in a bear hug.

"Welcome to our group. We will take you to our camp where you can get cleaned up and get some different clothes," he said, as he shook his head while eyeing the Nazi uniform. "That uniform may come in handy for some of our missions."

It took less than an hour of moderate hiking to reach the partisan's camp where Dave was offered food, a chance to wash and a change of clothes. He was also asked a multitude of questions. Dave quickly noticed the antenna that winded its way up into the trees and asked if it would be possible to send a message to the British. He was told that he would have to talk to their leader. An hour later, a short but very muscular man swaggered over to Dave and plopped down next to him.

"I am Ludwik Borkowski. I am the leader of this partisan force." He offered Dave a swig from his bottle. Dave could see that the leader was already a little drunk. Dave took a drink and wished that he hadn't. It burned all the way down and he was sure that if he could check his tonsils, they would be would be half burned away. He coughed and then sputtered. The commander roared with laughter.

"Don't you Canadians ever get good drink?" He stopped laughing and then sat in silence for a short time.

"I have been told that you would like to send a message to England." Dave nodded. "What would this message be about?" Ludwik inquired.

"I have information that has to get to American Lieutenant Colonel George Baker and I'm sure he will risk sending a plane in to pick me up as soon as he is contacted."

The commander turned to gaze at the camp as he sat whistling a song for a few seconds and then turned back to Dave.

"Alright, at three in the morning you will have three minutes and no more. Your American colonel will be notified ahead of time to be present," he said, and then arose and shuffled away like he had all the time in the world.

Dave was in the small lean-to that they called the communication center and when it was nearly three, the switch was thrown and the radio slowly came to life. Dave had never realized that it took so long for the tubes to warm up. He took the mike.

"This is Captain David Lysik, RCAF. I need to talk to Lt. Colonel Baker, over."

"I'm here, Captain. What have you got, son?"

"The fields are white and ripe for harvest."

"Are you sure you have enough?"

"My cup is running over."

"OK son, you stay put and we'll make arrangements. Pass me back to the radio op," Baker said sounding almost excited.

The radio operator gave the colonel the information that he needed in code and then flipped the switch and the radio went dead. Dave glanced at his watch and was surprised to see it had only taken slightly less than three minutes.

Dave made his way back to his billet, laid down and almost instantly fell asleep. He was awakened with a start by Ludwik. Dave couldn't believe that he had even slept but it was now late in the afternoon. He noticed that someone had graciously put several covers on him to help him keep warm.

"We must leave soon if we are to arrive at your pick-up spot on time, but first we will eat," Ludwig said, as he stood with a few others. Dave noticed that they were all armed.

"Where are we going?" Dave asked.

"It's probably better if you don't know, but it will take us several hours to get to our destination and when we get there we will wait for your colonel friend."

Dave couldn't figure out what the meal was and didn't care. Compared to the cabbage soup and small portion of bread he'd had to get used to in the camp, this was like a thanksgiving dinner with all the trimmings.

Several hours later, Dave's legs felt as though they could not make another stride and especially at the speed these guys moved, but he kept moving. They went through forests, meadows, fields and more forest. Finally, Ludwig gave the order to spread out and rest. No sooner had Dave sat down with his back to a tree, than he noticed a lake up ahead and saw two of the men uncover an inflatable dingy. Ludwig turned to Dave.

"My men will paddle you out on the lake." Ludwig said. "A float plane will land soon, pick you up and offload some supplies. The rest of us will act as a rear guard here under cover." Ludwig and Dave sat in a treed area and talked.

"So my young friend, do you have a wife or girlfriend back in Canada?" asked Ludwig.

"A wife and a child. We were married just a few months before I was sent to England. That was nearly..." he stopped to calculate the time. "My God, that was over two years ago! My wife had just given me the news that she was pregnant and so I guess I have a 2-year-old son or daughter now. Julia - that's my wife - figured it would be a boy, but I don't really know." Dave said earnestly, as Ludwik smiled.

"I, too had a wife when all this started. We lived near Bialystok and I was a farmer. We were happy and had three children - two boys and a little girl." Ludwig's demeanour turned hard. "One day, when I came home from a day's work in the fields, I found my wife, little girl and one of the boys gone. I found the other boy trembling in the loft. He had watched the SS beat, ravage and then lead the three away. I have never seen them since and I believe they have been killed by them Nazi pigs." Dave could see the loss and hatred in the man's eyes and somehow felt embarrassed that his own wife was back in Saskatchewan with their child, waiting for him.

"I'm sorry," Dave said, and the two sat silent for a long time.

A Purple Heart Bride
Chapter 13

Johnson, second in command of the Polish brigade, sent out two teams of two men each to scout around the lake to ensure that there were no German patrols in the area. They returned just after dark, assuring their leader that the lake was safe. Ludwik motioned and four of the men grabbed the dingy, two on each side and ran for the water. The leader signalled to Dave. Dave nodded and hurried into the water up to his knees and then rolled into the raft with the help of a couple of the brigade members in the craft. All four Polish men then began paddling, two on each side, heading toward the center of the lake.

It was nearly a half-hour later that they suddenly stopped paddling and Dave heard the deep drone of an aircraft engine up in the sky. One of the men shone a flashlight toward the sound and then extinguished it, repeating the procedure several times. Somehow the pilot was supposed to land near them but not on them. Dave was intrigued. He certainly wouldn't want to try a landing like this.

Minutes later, they heard the splash of the plane as it touched down and the engines slowed slightly. Dave could make out the white froth that the amphibious aircraft made in the water as it sprayed away from the hull of the plane. It made a slow semi-circle and almost came to stop, only a hundred feet from the raft. Dave recognized the

American PBY Catalina when it got closer and watched as crew members launched their own rubber raft, paddling out to the one Dave was in. They threw a couple of sacks filled with something into the raft and after Dave shook the hands of the Partisans and thanked them, the two Americans grasped his arms and pulled him into their raft. Dave moved to a corner of the raft and watched as the Partisans paddled into the dark and out of sight.

The Americans quickly paddled back to the PBY and then hoisted Dave into the plane. A few minutes later, after the pair of sailors had quickly climbed aboard, the plane was already picking up speed to take off in the direction it had come. The sailors stowed the raft and then directed Dave to the flight deck. The Catalina was now in the air and heading for England.

"Welcome aboard, Captain Lysik. Heard you've had some serious times," the pilot said. "I'm Lieutenant Colonel Jakes, US Navy. We'll be home in merry old England in about two and a half hours. In the meantime, we brought along some correspondence we thought you might like to read." He nodded to one of the crew and the sailor gave Dave a pouch. Dave opened it and found two bundles of letters. One was huge while the other had only three envelopes. He opened the first bundle and read.

Hi Captain,
If you're reading this, then I guess somehow

you must have escaped. Jack, Charley and me managed to get back to England with the help of Joseph and his men. Hey Captain, look me up when you get back to Canada, as I really think you will.

Your Tail Gunner

Billy

The other two letters in the bundle were from Jack and Charley and basically said the same thing with the notable exception of Jack reminding Dave of his invitation for a real Texas barbecue. Dave set them aside and picked up the other bundle. He could see by the writing that they were from Julia. He pulled off the elastic band that held them together, noticing that they were wrapped chronologically. Excitedly, he ripped open the first one and found a picture of a little boy. The little guy looked to be about a year old in the picture. He unfolded the letter that was with it.

Dear Dave,

Honey, they've told me you are missing in action and probably dead and I should stop sending you letters, but I don't believe it and I choose to believe you're just having a tough time getting back to us. Yes, <u>us</u>. Dave Jr. is already looking for his Dada and I tell him every day you will come home soon. I was up to P.A. last week and your parents are of the same mind. They said it would take a lot more than Hitler to stop you. We're being foolish, of course, but I feel

deep in my heart that you will come home. I'm
waiting until then. Kisses and hugs.
xoxoxoxoxoxoxoxoxoxoxoxo
Julia & Dave Jr.

Dave folded the letter and put it back in the envelope. Tears sneaked out and ran down over his cheek, which he wiped away with his hand. He didn't open any of the rest. He just sat there staring at the little boy. It was his little boy and the wonderful woman who was holding him was the beautiful lady he had married. Life was good again and in a few weeks, he would be home with them.

When Dave got off the plane, he was taken to a meeting with Colonel Baker. When he passed the canisters to him, he was surprised that there was no fanfare, no excitement. In fact, the colonel barely glanced at the two small containers and without even checking the contents, threw the canisters in his desk drawer. He suggested that they have coffee. Dave was curious and even a little annoyed.

"Aren't you going to have G2 study them?" Dave asked.

"Actually we've got conclusive reconnaissance of the camp and the folks you dropped in before your crash have fed us with detailed information on the fission labs which we've already bombed to oblivion, so..." he held his hands up to simulate defeat. "We will want you in a debriefing though, considering that you went through one of their concentration camps." He glanced at Dave. "I'm sure you can give us a vivid picture of what is going on there." Dave wasn't sure he could put his disgust with what he had seen into words, but he would try.

"I was in a death camp," Dave said quietly.

"What was that?"

"It was only one of many *death* camps," he said, emphasizing the word death. They're killing Jewish people by the thousands, or maybe millions - but they don't just kill them. They abuse them in as grotesque a way as they can, while accomplishing it in an almost assembly-line fashion. They steal everything they have and then, if they haven't died already, they gas them and incinerate the bodies. They are killing them - men, women and children, young and old - all innocent." Dave broke down sobbing. The colonel patted him on the back.

"OK, OK - You've had a rough time of it." The colonel gently patted him on the back again. When Dave had regained his composure, the colonel called in a soldier from the reception area.

"Corporal! Take the captain over to the Royal hotel and help him find his room and make sure he has everything he needs," he said, sympathetically. "Dave, get some rest. We'll call for you, ah, probably tomorrow sometime. We'll get you debriefed and then send you home for some R&R." The corporal escorted Dave out to a gray Plymouth and delivered him to the hotel.

It was nearly a month later when Dave stepped off the train in Saskatoon. Julia, carrying Dave Jr., hurried towards Dave and the happy couple embraced. Julia was crying tears of joy and Dave's eyes were moist, also.

Dave stared at his son while Julia put the little fellow down. Dave marveled that he was standing on his own. Then, with some urging from his mother, Dave Jr.'s first word to his father was "Dada."

Dave scooped the boy into his arms and gave him kisses. Dave Jr. just giggled.

190